*To my friends and family who may now be gone,
but will never be forgotten!*

Praise for Chris Cavender's Pizza Mysteries!

Killer Crust
"Tasty . . . this is another fun pizza romp."
—*Publishers Weekly*

Rest in Pizza
"These cozy pizza mysteries have been truly outstanding and this particular one will leave the reader once again wanting a whole lot more of the great writing and cool plots that Chris Cavender continues to serve."
—*Suspense Magazine*

A Pizza to Die For
"Just like a pizza with all your favorite toppings, this series will satisfy even the most finicky cozy readers. Fans of Laura Childs and Joanne Fluke will most likely enjoy this series as well."
—*RT Book Reviews*

Pepperoni Pizza Can Be Murder
"The small-town setting, the small-business focus and the relationship between sisters Maddy and Eleanor are all reminiscent of Joanne Fluke's Hannah Swensen mysteries."
—*Booklist*

A Slice of Murder
"Pizza lovers will relish Cavender's delightful first in a new cozy series . . . A lively pace and a thrilling climax."
—*Publishers Weekly*

"The camaraderie of the Timber Ridge, NC, sisters is reminiscent of Nancy Martin's Blackbird siblings."
—*Library Journal*

"A delightful mystery—as filling as a big slice of warm pizza."
—*Armchair Interviews*

Books by Chris Cavender

A SLICE OF MURDER

PEPPERONI PIZZA CAN BE MURDER

A PIZZA TO DIE FOR

REST IN PIZZA

KILLER CRUST

THE MISSING DOUGH

Published by Kensington Publishing Corporation

THE MISSING DOUGH

CHRIS CAVENDER

KENSINGTON BOOKS
www.kensingtonbooks.com

KENSINGTON BOOKS are published by

Kensington Publishing Corp.
119 West 40th Street
New York, NY 10018

All Kensington titles, imprints, and distributed lines are available at special quantity discounts for bulk purchases for sales promotion, premiums, fund-raising, educational, or institutional use. Special book excerpts or customized printings can also be created to fit specific needs. For details, write or phone the office of the Kensington Special Sales Manager: Attn. Special Sales Department. Kensington Publishing Corp., 119 West 40th Street, New York, NY 10018. Phone: 1-800-221-2647.

Kensington and the K logo Reg. U.S. Pat. & TM Off.

ISBN-13: 978-0-7582-7155-6
ISBN-10: 0-7582-7155-7
First Kensington Hardcover Edition: December 2013
First Kensington Mass Market Edition: January 2015

eISBN-13: 978-0-7582-9154-7
eISBN-10: 0-7582-9154-X
First Kensington Electronic Edition: December 2013

10 9 8 7 6 5 4 3 2 1

Printed in the United States of America

Da mihi sis crustum Etruscum cum omnibus in eo.

(I'll have a pizza with everything on it.)
http://freepages.rootsweb.ancestry.com/
~wakefield/funlatin.html

Quiquid latine dictum sit altum viditur.

(Whatever is said in Latin sounds profound.)
http://freepages.rootsweb.ancestry.com/
~wakefield/funlatin.html

Chapter 1

"Maddy, I'm not leaving here until you promise to give me another chance!"

I heard the man shouting all the way from the kitchen of my pizza parlor, A Slice of Delight. It was just ten minutes since we'd opened our doors for the day. I'd been hoping for a quiet shift, but it was clear that I'd have no such luck today. What was going on with my sister now, and who was yelling at her? Whatever was happening, it sounded as though she could use some help. Maddy usually handled the front dining room with no trouble, along with our two part-timers, Greg and Josh, but she was up there alone at the moment, and I needed to see if I could back her up, no matter what the circumstances.

As I hurried up front, I grabbed our security system on the way, an aluminum baseball bat we'd played with as kids. Thankfully, the dining room was empty except for Maddy and a man I thought I'd seen the last of years before.

"Grant, what are you doing here?" I asked as I pointed the business end of the bat toward him like a spear.

"Hello, Eleanor," he said with that greasy way he had about him, lowering his voice and doing his best to smile at me. There was no love lost between the two of us, and I didn't even try to fake a smile in return.

Years ago, Maddy had married Grant Whitmore on the rebound from a bad breakup, though I'd done my best to talk her out of it at the time. The man was almost a cliché: tall, dark, and handsome, a troubled loner that some women found irresistible. I wasn't talking about me, but clearly, some women reveled in his attention. Maddy had fallen for him, and hard, until fourteen months into their marriage she'd caught him cheating with their next-door neighbor. It wasn't all that surprising to me that Maddy had missed his mother more than she had her straying husband. She and her mother-in-law had formed a strong bond that had surpassed the marriage, and the two women had kept in touch long after the dissolution of Maddy's marriage to the woman's son.

"You didn't answer my question, Grant," I said as calmly as I could manage. "Why are you here?"

Maddy looked over at me and frowned. "I can handle this, Sis."

"There's no doubt in my mind that you can, but why should you have all of the fun? If it were possible, I might even like him less than you do." I was normally a pretty levelheaded woman, but this guy was on my Trouble list, a place that no one in their right mind would ever want to be.

Grant tried to wield his questionable charm on me. "Your sister is right, Eleanor. We don't need your input. We're doing just fine without you."

That was the wrong thing to say to Maddy, and I knew it as I tried to suppress a smile. Grant realized it as well from the instant the statement left his lips, but it was too late for him to take it back.

Maddy answered, "Grant, I don't need your support, your permission, or your acknowledgment of anything I say, think, or do. I threw you out for a reason, and if you think there's a whisper of a chance you are getting back into my life, you are sadly mistaken. I'm happy, I'm engaged, and I'm well rid of you." She looked at me, then glanced at the baseball bat still in my hands. "Could I borrow that?"

"By all means," I said as I handed the bat to her. "But don't hog all of the fun for yourself. I want a shot at him after you're finished."

"What makes you think that there will be anything left after I take my turn?" she asked with her most wicked of grins.

"Ladies, I can see that I've caught you at a bad time," Grant said as he started backing slowly toward the front door. "There's no need to resolve this all at once. There will be plenty of time. I'm not going anywhere. We'll talk again later."

"Or just maybe we're finished here, once and for all," Maddy said. "I meant what I said. There's nothing left to talk about."

Grant made his way to the door and then hesitated before leaving. "Madeline, you can protest all you want to, but I know there's still a spark for me buried somewhere deep in your heart."

"Grant, it's amazing the number of things you think you know about me but don't," Maddy said. She suddenly lunged with the bat, grinned again, and he left quickly.

"What was that all about?" I asked her after we were sure he wasn't coming back.

"What can I say? I guess I'm really just *that* irresistible," she answered with a grin.

"Really? You don't think there's something else going on here?"

"Of course I do," she replied. "Grant is up to something, and I doubt that it's because he is in Timber Ridge to win back my heart. There's only one way to find out, though. I'm calling Sharon."

"Do you really think your former mother-in-law will tell you what her son is up to?" I asked as my sister got out her cell phone.

"Are you kidding? Sharon was hoping to lose

him in the divorce instead of me." Maddy listened to her phone for a minute and then hung up. "I got her machine; she's not there. I'll try again later. In the meantime, what say we put this behind us and get ready for our first customer?"

"Aren't you going to call Bob and tell him what just happened?" I asked. Bob Lemon was a local attorney and, more importantly, Maddy's fiancé. "I've got a hunch he might like to know that someone is trying to woo his betrothed."

Maddy glanced at her watch. "Bob knows all about Grant, so there's no way he'll be threatened by anything my ex has to say to me. Besides, he's in court right now. I'll tell him this evening at the festival. I'm glad we're closing the pizzeria at six so we can go this year, too."

"Hey, we only have a Founders Day Festival once a year," I said. "Besides, with all of the street vendors peddling their specialties, it's not like we'd sell much pizza anyway. It was one of Joe's favorite things about this place, you know."

"Oh, you don't have to remind me. I remember that crazy woodsman's costume he wore one year. I thought Grizzly Adams had come to town."

"My dear husband had a unique sense of humor, didn't he?" I asked.

Maddy nodded and then stared at me for a few seconds before she spoke again. "You know, you aren't nearly as sad as you used to be when you talk about him these days, Eleanor. Is it because David Quinton's in your life?"

I thought about it and then admitted, "You're probably right. Joe's been gone awhile now, and I'm doing my best to let go of the pain of losing him and focus more on the wonderful life we had together. I admit that David has helped me do it."

"By being in your life?" Maddy asked.

"Sure, that's true in and of itself, but my boyfriend loves to hear stories about Joe, and some of the stunts he used to pull. I swear, I believe that the two of them would have been great friends if they'd ever had a chance to meet."

"Well, they *do* have something in common," Maddy said. "They both managed to fall for you."

"And you can't argue with good taste, can you?" I asked her with a smile.

At that moment, four older fellows came into the Slice together. To my knowledge, they'd never been in my pizzeria before, and judging by the way they looked around, it was a pretty sure bet. They weren't exactly in their element.

As Maddy seated them, I asked, "What brings you gentlemen here on this fine and beautiful day?"

"They shut down the Liar's Table at Mickey's in Bower," one of them said, clearly more than a little disgruntled by the fact. "We're trying new places this week, until they're finished remodeling."

"Did you just say Liar's Table?" Maddy asked. "What exactly does that mean?"

One of the men grinned at her as he ran a hand

through his full head of silver hair. "It's a time-honored name reserved for a group of regulars who tend to exaggerate their stories just a touch to make them a tad more vivid to the listener."

"Exaggerate?" a shiny-domed companion asked. "That's just about the nicest way of being called a liar I've heard yet."

"Give me time, Jed. I'll see what else I can come up with," his friend replied.

"Don't encourage him," a third man said. As Maddy offered them all menus, he held his hand up and said, "Don't worry about those; we know what we want. If this place is anything like the one I used to go to back when I had a full head of hair, give us a large kitchen-sink pizza and four sodas."

"When did you start ordering for us, Henry?" one of the other men asked.

"Forget that," Jed said. "I want to know how you can remember as far back as when you actually had hair."

"Yeah. I resent the implication that I can't make up my own mind," the heretofore silent one chimed in.

Henry looked at them each in turn and then said, "Excuse me. I didn't mean to be presumptuous. So, what kind of pizza would you three like?"

They mulled it over and finally decided that Henry had been right all along. After they placed their order, I went back into the kitchen to prepare it. Maddy and I liked fully loaded pizzas ourselves, using every topping we could get our hands on, so I could make one in my sleep. As it made its way through the conveyor oven we used, I had to wonder about Grant's earlier visit to the Slice. Was he really there to get back in my sister's life, or was there something more ominous behind his sudden appearance? I had to believe the latter, but only time would tell. I just hoped that he'd been bluffing when he said that he wasn't going to give up easily.

Our lives were plenty complicated enough without having one of Maddy's ex-husbands showing up and making trouble for all of us.

"It's really beautiful, isn't it?" I asked David Quinton as I held his hand later that evening when we first arrived at the festival.

The promenade where my pizzeria was located had been spruced up for the festival, with tiny white Christmas lights spread around the trees spaced throughout the broad brick square. Even the World War II cannon had pretty twinkly little lights on it, but the biggest center of attraction of all was the obelisk. With a shape that was a duplicate of the Washington Monument, it was a scaled-down version, an eighteen-foot-high memorial to the men and women who had founded Timber Ridge. Their names still dominated our town, with Lincolns, Murphys, Penneys, and even Swifts and

Spencers spread throughout the region, and there were most likely more folks with ties to the original founders living all around me than otherwise. What I loved most about the focus on the monument to our heritage was that the gray sentinel was bathed in an ever-changing floodlight of colors, and I wondered how they'd managed it.

"Would you like to dance, Eleanor?" David asked me as we neared one of the two stages set up on opposite ends of the square. They were far enough apart to be isolated from each other for the most part, but every now and then music from the bluegrass musicians on the other side drifted toward the stage near us, where a cover band was playing some of my favorite songs from my youth, a soundtrack of my life growing up.

"Why don't we get some barbeque first?" I suggested. It wasn't that I didn't enjoy dancing with my boyfriend, even if there was already a crowded floor of dancers, but it had been quite a while since I'd had lunch.

"I completely get the logic of feeding you first, but the offer's open for the rest of the night," he said with a smile. "But the next time, you have to ask me."

"You've got yourself a deal."

We made our way to one of the three barbeque sellers set up on the perimeter of the promenade, and I nodded to a few of my customers who were working behind the counter.

An older woman with a ready smile laughed the second she saw me approach. "Eleanor Swift! Who would have thought that I'd ever have the chance to serve you instead of the other way around?" Linda Tuesday said from behind the table.

"From those heavenly aromas coming from behind you, I wouldn't suggest trying to stop me. Is your husband cooking tonight?" Linda's husband, Manny, worked the pit at a barbeque place in Lincoln as his regular job, and he was a legend around our part for his skills in slow cooking.

"Try to keep him away from it," she said with a wry grin. "That man was born with barbeque sauce in his veins, and a fondness for cooking perfect pork barbeque that goes beyond obsession."

"And it's a good thing for the rest of us," I said. I didn't even have to glance at the menu printed on bright green posterboard. "Linda, we'll take two pulled specials, and do me a favor and sneak a bite of bark on my plate." Almost as an afterthought, I turned to David and asked, "Oops. Is that all right with you? I get kind of carried away when I'm around barbeque this good."

"Sure, it's fine with me, but if you're going to order for me, you're going to have to buy, Eleanor," he said with a grin.

"I like this one," Linda said as she looked at David and added another burst of laughter. "This one might just be a keeper. Or is it too soon to tell yet?"

"He's still on probation, but it's looking good so far," I said with a laugh of my own. Linda had that effect on me, and I always loved it when she came into the Slice.

"It's good to know that I haven't flunked out yet," David said good-naturedly as he started to reach for his wallet.

"Hey, what do you think you're doing, mister?" I said. "Put that away. This is my treat, remember?"

"Sorry. I forgot myself for just a second," he said.

Linda dished us up two plates brimming with pulled pork barbeque, baked beans, potato salad, slaw, and a good handful of french fries. Except for the barbeque itself, the portions weren't overwhelming, just a little more than a taste of each, but it was the only way you could get the full experience of the meal. We took our plates, along with the sweet tea that came with them, and found a bench that had just freed up under one of the nearby trees. Sitting spots were at a premium at the moment, even with the extra benches and chairs brought in just for the event, and we were lucky to grab one.

As we balanced our plates on our laps and began to eat, David took a bite of the barbeque, savored it for a few seconds, and then asked me, "What makes this so good? It doesn't even need any sauce."

"That's the work of a master," I said. "You can taste the smoke in every bite, can't you?"

David nodded, sampled a small bite of baked beans, and then asked me, "I heard you ask for bark. Is that the dark piece right there?"

I picked up the bark-edged piece of pulled pork with my fingers and smiled. "It's from the outside layer, and it's where the smoke and flavor are concentrated the most. It's not for everyone, but there's nothing like it as far as I'm concerned. Want a taste?"

"Sure. Why not?"

I offered a bit to David, who took it and took the smallest bite possible. "Wow, that's intense."

I had to laugh. "Hey, I told you that it's not for everybody."

"If it's all the same to you, I think I'll stick with this," he said.

After we finished eating, we found a trash can and tossed away our plates and cups. "How about that dance now?" David asked.

"I thought you were going to leave it up to me to ask the next time."

"I lied," he said with a grin.

"You're not going to stop asking until I agree to a dance, are you?"

"What can I say? I was born to boogie," he said with a smile.

"Then lead on."

We moved toward the crowd of dancers, and I

had to admit, it felt good being in his arms once we carved out a place for ourselves. I'd missed that close contact with someone after Joe died, and it had taken me a long time to allow myself to enjoy it again.

I was just getting into the rhythm of the music when I heard a commotion not far away from us. The second I heard Maddy's voice, I broke free of David's grasp and started toward the ruckus.

Clearly, there was trouble, and if my sister was involved, I wasn't going to let myself be very far away.

When we got to Maddy, I saw that the crowd had parted and that Bob and Grant were in some kind of standoff, while Maddy was trying to get in between them.

David stepped forward, and asked Bob intently, "Do you need any help?" as he stared at Grant. I'd neglected to tell my boyfriend about my sister's ex, and I was beginning to regret the lapse.

Bob's face was flushed, but he shook his head at the offer. "Thanks, but he's not worth the effort from one of us, let alone both."

"What happened?" I asked Maddy, who for once looked positively flustered by what was going on.

"Bob and I were dancing when Grant tried to cut in," she explained. "At my urging, Bob refused, but Grant wouldn't take no for an answer. He pushed Bob in the back, and my fiancé pushed him right back."

"I never laid a hand on him. That was someone else shoving him in the back. I was minding my own business when he assaulted me," Grant complained loudly to the audience we were all attracting. "I'm going to have this man arrested for it, and I expect you all to be witnesses."

He couldn't have broken up the crowd any more effectively if he'd used tear gas on them. Soon enough, it was just the five of us standing there, and when I got closer to Grant, I could easily smell the liquor on him. I knew that they sold beer in some of the tents to fairgoers, but it seemed to me that he'd been drinking something quite a bit harder than that.

"You're drunk," I said. "Go back to your hotel room and sleep it off. Nobody's going to say a word in your defense."

"You think you've won," Grant said as he glared at Bob and shook a finger in his face. "But you're wrong. She was mine before, and she'll be mine again."

"Over my dead body," Bob said.

"If you insist, that can certainly be arranged," Grant said, being careful not to slur his words, though he had a bit of difficulty with *certainly*.

"Is that a threat?" Bob asked as he looked up at Grant and took a step closer to the man. Maddy's ex had a good six inches on Bob and at least thirty pounds of muscle. It was clear that he was in much better shape, but that didn't deter Bob in the least.

"It's a promise," Grant said.

David somehow managed to step between them and faced Grant. "Maybe you ought to just move along. It's pretty clear that nobody wants you here."

"And who exactly are you?" Grant asked as he focused on my boyfriend.

"Me? I'm nobody, just someone trying to make the peace. We don't want to ruin this evening for all of these other folks, now, do we?"

"I don't give a rat's left whisker for the lot of you," he said, some of his words now beginning to slur in earnest. "Butt out, bub."

Grant suddenly made a lunge in David's direction, and Bob pulled David back half a step. As he did, Grant had no one to support him, and he suddenly fell forward on his face. He was so sloshed that he hadn't had the foresight to break his fall with his hands, and when he stood up again, his nose was bloody from its impact with the bricks of the promenade. "He hit me!" Grant screamed to no one in particular.

"I did no such thing," Bob said calmly, though he didn't look displeased that Grant had managed to bloody his own nose. "You can ask anyone."

"Why should I bother? You already told me that they'll all just lie for you." Grant spotted Police Chief Kevin Hurley just then, who was making the rounds of the fair and had no doubt heard the disturbance. "Officer, arrest that man," Grant said as he pointed to Bob.

"Why on earth would I do that? What's going on?" Kevin asked. "Is there a problem here?"

"That man struck me," Grant said, his voice slightly muffled as he held a handkerchief against his nose, trying to stop the bleeding.

Chief Hurley looked at Bob as he raised one eyebrow. "Counselor, is that true?"

"He was taking a swing at David, so I stepped in," Bob explained.

"To hit him?" the chief asked, a little surprise slipping into his question as he asked it.

"Of course not," I said. "Grant fell down all by himself. We all saw it. He didn't need any help from any of us. He's clearly plastered."

"Eleanor, I don't believe I asked you for your take on this," the chief said.

"No, but I'm sure you just hadn't gotten around to it yet," I said. The chief and I had had more than our share of problems in the past, dating back to our high school years when we'd gone out briefly, but I wanted to make this go away quickly so we could enjoy the rest of the night. "This is Maddy's ex-husband," I explained, "and he's been blustering around town all day that he's here to get her back, something she continues to tell him is impossible."

"Is that true?" the chief asked Maddy.

"I couldn't have said it any better myself," Maddy said. She looked at me and grinned as she added, "And you know that I would have done it if my big sister had been able to let me have a chance on my own."

"Sorry about that," I said with a smile of my own that showed I wasn't the least bit repentant for my actions.

"You're forgiven," she replied with a nod.

"Okay, I've heard enough." The chief turned to Grant and said, "You've got two choices, the way I see it. You can move along peacefully right now and leave these good folks alone to enjoy the celebration, or you can spend the night sobering up in one of my jail cells."

Grant snapped out, "Why am I not surprised that you'd side with them? Are you in their pockets, too?"

"Excuse me?" the chief asked in the near silence that seemed to surround him for a moment. Though the question had been posed in a restricted voice, all of those around us knew that Grant was on dangerous ground at the moment.

"Never mind," Grant said as he started away. Before he could fade into the crowd, though, he said to the group of us, "This isn't over."

"For your sake, it had better be," the chief said.

After Grant had disappeared into the crowd, Bob spoke up. "Thank you, but I had things under control here."

Before Chief Hurley could respond, Maddy said, "Of course you did. Now, are we going to finish our dance, or am I going to have to ask the chief of police instead?"

"It would be my pleasure," Bob said as he took Maddy into his arms.

Chief Hurley looked at me, shrugged, and then went back to his rounds of the festival.

David said, "Our dance wasn't finished either, as I recall."

"Then by all means, let's dance," I said.

As we moved in time with the music, David whispered in my ear, "Why do I have the feeling that this isn't over?"

"Probably because you've been around Maddy and me too much lately," I said.

"Too much? Never. I dispute your claim that there could ever be too much contact with you."

"And Maddy, as well?" I asked softly, for his ears only.

"Let's just say that I'm glad I chose the right sister," David answered. When I didn't respond, he leaned back and asked, "Are you telling me that you're going to let me get away with that?"

"What can I say? I'm feeling pretty forgiving all the way around tonight. Now, are we going to talk, or are we going to dance?"

"Yap with you or hold you in my arms? That's not even a fair fight," he said as he pulled me a little closer. After that, I didn't spend too much more time worrying about Grant and why he'd reappeared in our lives.

For now, for that moment in time, I was just content being exactly where I was, keeping the company I was keeping, and being a part of the life of Timber Ridge, North Carolina.

Chapter 2

"That band is really good, isn't it?" David asked me a little later as we took a break from dancing and stood near the group currently playing onstage. I'd been on my feet all afternoon at the Slice, and while I loved to dance just fine, it was nice to rest every now and then.

"They are," I agreed. "The lead singer's really pretty, isn't she?"

"I guess so, but she's still not as pretty as you are," David answered.

"That's the perfect response; you know that, don't you?"

"How so?" David asked, his attention rarely leaving the stage.

"If you'd said you hadn't noticed her, I would

have known you were lying, and if you'd agreed too enthusiastically, then we would have had a problem there, too."

"Hey, what can I say?" he asked as he turned to look at me. "I just got lucky."

I laughed as I turned my attention back to the stage again. The singer *was* good, a sultry brunette who hit all of the right notes, and the guitar player backing her up had a knack as well. The drummer was holding them back a little, at least in my opinion, but they were still a cut above our usual town offerings when it came to music on the promenade.

I was still watching them play when David touched my arm lightly. "Eleanor, look over there."

"Where?"

I followed his pointed finger to an area of trees on the outside of the promenade. At first I couldn't make out who was arguing, but it took me just a second to realize that one of them was good old Grant. He seemed to have a nose for an argument tonight, the pun fully intended. He was with another man, and it was pretty clear they weren't happy with each other at all. Heated words were exchanged, and then the stranger walked away. Grant tried to follow him, but he gave up when the female lead singer said from the stage, "We're going to take a little break for the fireworks right now. We hope you grant us the time and enjoy the show."

Grant's head snapped around when he heard a

variation of his name coming from the stage, and I could swear that I saw the singer nod and motion for him to come backstage when they made eye contact. This clearly upset the guitarist, and I wondered what was going on.

I was about to see if I could find out when Maddy came over to us, Bob in tow.

"After the fireworks are over, what do you think about the four of us buying more food and eating it on your front porch, Eleanor? This crowd's getting to be too much for our tastes."

"It sounds great to me. That snack didn't fill me up. What do you think?" I asked David.

"I'm all for it," he answered, just as a cup of beer came flying straight for us out of the crowd. It managed to spill onto each of us a little, but Bob took the lion's share of the liquid barrage.

"I'll kill him," Bob said uncharacteristically as he started off into the crowd.

"Hang on a second. Who exactly are you going to kill?" David asked as he put a hand on Bob's arm. The two men had become friends after being in such close proximity because of us, and I loved how they looked out for each other.

"You know as well as I do that Grant Whitmore threw that beer at us," Bob said as he tried to pull his arm free.

David wasn't about to let go, though. "I don't doubt that you're right, but we can't prove it, can we? Bob, think it through. He *wants* you to come after him. Don't give him the satisfaction."

Bob looked hard at David for a full second, and then said, "Do you think I'm afraid of *him?*"

"Of course not. But you know as well as I do that you've got to pick your battles, and this isn't one of them."

Bob thought about that for a moment longer, and when he pulled his arm out of David's grip, my boyfriend didn't fight him on it. He could see that the fight had gone out of him, at least for now.

"I have to go home and change," Bob said a little sullenly.

"We all do," David answered with a laugh, trying to make light of it. He turned to Maddy and me and said, "Tell you what. Why don't you pick up the food, and we'll all meet back at Eleanor's place. How does that sound?"

"Great," Maddy said quickly. "Bob, you don't mind if I ride with Eleanor, do you?"

"What? No, not at all," Bob said. "David, do you need a ride?"

"I drove over here by myself, but if you'd like some company, I can always pick my car up tomorrow."

"Nonsense. No one has to babysit me. I'm over that fool. I'll see you all later."

After the men were gone and Maddy and I were standing in line for food, my sister said, "Eleanor, I've got a bad feeling about this. I should have gone with him."

"You can probably still catch up with him, if you really want to," I said.

She thought about it and then finally said, "No, he wouldn't like that. Bob's got a great deal of pride, and sometimes I have to tiptoe around his ego so I don't accidentally bruise it. It may not show, but the man does have his flaws."

"Unlike the two of us," I said with a laugh.

"We *are* pretty perfect, aren't we?" she asked.

"We are as far as I'm willing to admit to the outside world," I answered. "Don't worry. Bob and David will be fine."

"I'm sure you're right. I just don't like the way Grant threatened us all."

"Do you think he'd actually follow through with it?" I asked. "He never seemed like the dangerous type to me when you were married."

"No, but he's always had a bit of a cruel streak in him, and who knows how much he's changed since we were together?"

"Maddy, we can call Kevin Hurley if you'd like." I knew that Grant, and her marriage to him, were both sore spots for her.

"No, I'm just being silly. I'm sure that they'll be fine."

It was our turn to order next, and we ended up buying enough food to feed an army. I was happy that Manny was used to cooking in such large quantities. After all the food they'd served that evening, there was still plenty left over for our little impromptu late-night picnic.

But if I were being honest with myself, I'd be relieved once we were all together again, sitting on my front porch and enjoying the meal, away from the crowds and, more importantly, a pushy ex-husband.

As a matter of course, Maddy and I kept clothes at each other's places in case we had one of our impromptu overnight visits, so we went straight to my place so we could shower and change. The re-modeled Craftsman-style bungalow where I lived was home to me for so many reasons. Joe and I had invested a great deal of sweat equity into it, bringing it back to its former glory one step at a time. It was the one place on earth, even more than the pizzeria, where I still felt his presence the most, and that was a very good thing indeed.

After Maddy and I had showered and changed, we set up a small table on the porch, reheated the beans and barbeque, and then added the potato salad and slaw to the offering. The table seemed to groan under all the weight on it, but I knew that wouldn't last for long.

David's headlights finally illuminated the porch, and he joined us.

"Where's Bob?" he asked as he looked around.

"He's not here yet," Maddy said. "Should we be worried about him?"

"No, of course not. I'm sure he's fine," David said as he glanced in my direction and raised a sin-gle eyebrow out of Maddy's line of sight.

"Of course he is," I said. "So, what do you think?

Should we wait or go ahead and grab some plates and start eating?"

"We should wait," Maddy said at the same time David answered, "I say we go ahead and eat."

We all laughed as Maddy reached for her cell phone. After a minute, she closed it abruptly. "That's odd. He's not answering."

"Maybe he's too busy driving over to pick up his phone," I said.

David shrugged as he put the plate he'd grabbed down on the rail. "There's no use standing around here speculating about it. I'll go see what's keeping him."

"You don't have to do that," I said, but Maddy put a hand on his shoulder. "Thanks. I would really appreciate that."

"I'm happy to do it." David was two steps from his car when another set of headlights started down the street toward us. Was it Bob or someone else? As the car approached, it slowed down, and I was more than a little relieved when I saw that it was indeed Maddy's fiancé.

As he got out of his car, David grinned at him. "I was just about to start up a search party for you, buddy. Where have you been?"

"I had to take a really long shower to get all of the beer out of my hair," he said. "I still can't believe what a jerk your ex-husband was tonight, Maddy. What did you ever see in the man?"

"Things that clearly were never there," she said

as she put her arm in his. "Bob, I'm really glad you're here."

"There's nowhere else I'd rather be," he said as he patted her arm. "I don't know about the rest of you, but I'm starving." He looked at the still-empty plates and asked, "You didn't wait for me, did you?"

David replied quickly, "I didn't want to, but they made me. You know how these two ladies are when they stand united."

"They are indeed a formidable force," Bob admitted. "Well, now that I'm here, let's eat, shall we?"

We took turns dishing out our plates, and Maddy went around pouring servings of sweet tea. It was the perfect combination of good food and fine fellowship, a night to be cherished and savored like the best of wines. I loved the memories we were creating tonight, adding to the ones I cherished as the best times of my life; this was fast becoming a real keeper.

"Does anybody want any more food?" I asked as I got up to survey what was still left. There was probably just enough barbeque and slaw left over to make one small sandwich; we'd really done a fine job of demolishing nearly all of the food we'd bought at the fair.

"I'm full," David said, and the rest of us agreed with him.

"Then I've still got a late-night snack after you all go home," I said as I started to collect the containers so I could pop them in the fridge.

"Can you honestly eat after all we've just had?" David asked.

"Maybe not right now, but give me enough time, and I'll manage just fine."

"Ladies, why don't the two of you keep your seats? David and I will clean up," Bob announced. "You two deserve a break."

I grinned as I quickly sat back down. "That's one order from a man that I'd be delighted to obey. Should Maddy and I supervise you, or should we just enjoy the evening while you two take care of things?"

I don't know what Bob's answer might have been had we not been interrupted just then, but suddenly it didn't seem to matter one way or the other about his generous offer.

A police cruiser came down my street in an awful hurry, and though there were no sirens wailing or lights flashing, it was clear that something was not entirely right with the cozy little town of Timber Ridge, North Carolina.

The second Chief Hurley got out of his car, I knew that something bad had happened, and worse yet, there was no doubt in my mind that it involved the four of us.

"What's going on, Kevin?" I asked as I hurried down the porch steps toward him. "Did something happen?"

"Why do you ask that?" he asked as he stopped in his tracks.

"You're clearly a man on a mission," I said, "and it's pretty obvious that something's wrong."

"I wish I could say that you're wrong, but I can't. How long have the four of you been here on the porch?"

"You're not going to tell us what happened first?" Maddy asked.

"If you have any hope of getting anything out of me, you'll have to answer my questions first," he said in a voice that offered no compromises.

"Hold on there just one second—" Bob said, but I interrupted him. I knew the attorney would want to control this situation, but it wasn't the time for us to dig our heels in.

"We won't gain anything by holding back." I turned to the police chief and said, "After we left the fair, we came here and had a little impromptu picnic right out here in front of everybody. We don't have anything to hide."

Was it my imagination, or did he look a little relieved by my admission? "Let me ask you this. Did the four of you come here together, or were you each in separate vehicles?"

"Maddy and I came together, but David and Bob drove their own cars. We all had to shower and change because someone in the crowd at the celebration threw a cup of beer on us as we were leaving."

"So, you two alibi each other," Kevin said to Maddy and me, and then he turned to Bob and David. "How about the two of you? Is there anyone who can confirm that you did exactly what Eleanor just claimed you did?"

David shook his head, as did Bob. The attorney said, "Chief, we don't have airtight alibis, if that's what you're asking. No matter what Eleanor says, I'm afraid that I'm going to have to insist that you tell us what this is about before we answer any more questions."

The police chief considered the request for twenty seconds and then shrugged as he said, "I don't know what harm it will do telling you now, since you'll hear about it soon enough." He turned to Maddy and said, "I hate to be the one to tell you this, but someone killed your ex-husband at the fair tonight."

Chapter 3

"He's really dead?" Maddy asked incredulously. The look of shock on her face would have been impossible to fake. "Kevin, how can he be gone? We all just saw him not an hour and a half ago."

"I'm afraid it's true enough," Kevin said. "There's no doubt about it."

"And you think one of us did it?" Bob asked angrily.

"Bob, everyone in Timber Ridge knows that you were fighting with him at the celebration tonight," the chief said, "so save your righteous indignation for somebody else. If you'll recall, I had to break you two up before you started brawling on the promenade in the middle of the fair, like a couple of teenagers."

"It wasn't nearly as bad as all that," Bob said.

Kevin bit his lower lip for a second before speaking again. "If Grant Whitmore hadn't just been murdered tonight I might agree with you, but as it stands, you have to know that you're at the top of my list."

Bob just shrugged. If he was particularly upset about being accused of murder, he wasn't showing it. "If you're here to arrest me, I'll be happy to go along with you willingly."

"He might come peacefully, but *I'm* not making any promises," Maddy said. "Chief, I'm truly sorry to hear that someone killed Grant, but Bob didn't do it."

"How can you say that for sure, Maddy? Eleanor told me herself that you split up coming over here."

"I know Bob," Maddy said. The shock of her ex-husband's death was finally sinking in. "How exactly did he die?"

"It wasn't a very pleasant way to go. Someone stabbed him in the heart with a barbeque skewer," he said as he looked at the foil-wrapped feast we'd all just had. "Did you folks happen to have some barbeque at the fair tonight?"

"Of course we did," I said. "Along with just about everyone else on the promenade. It was just about all there was to eat there, remember?"

"But you got more to bring here with you when you left, didn't you?" Kevin asked.

"We didn't steal a skewer, though," David said.

The police chief didn't respond to that, so I had to wonder if he'd already made up his mind about Bob. Kevin was usually a good cop, but when he got his sights set on one suspect, it took some monumental evidence to get him to change his mind. That was usually where Maddy and I came in. We'd been known to dig into a murder or two in the past, and it was looking more and more as though we were going to be forced into duty again. Not that I minded. I wasn't about to let my sister's fiancé take a fall for something he hadn't done.

"David, what exactly was *your* contact with the deceased?" the police chief asked.

"Are you honestly asking me if *I* had a motive?" my boyfriend asked.

"At the moment I'm just looking for information," he said.

"David was acting as a peacemaker, not an instigator," I said, trying my best to defend him. It was only a second later that I realized what I might be implying about Bob. "Chief, you might not know this yet, but we weren't the only folks angry with Grant tonight."

He was clearly unhappy to learn that I might know something that he might not yet. "What are you talking about, Eleanor? If this is a ploy to distract me, I'm telling you right now that it's not going to work."

"It's the truth," I said. "David and I saw Grant arguing with a stranger during the show, and when the cover band playing onstage took a break for the fireworks, it was pretty clear that the lead singer wanted to talk to Maddy's ex-husband, and just as obvious that the guitar player wasn't pleased about the prospect."

"Eleanor, you can't be serious."

"You bet she is," David said. "I saw that myself. Why aren't you talking to them instead of coming here and grilling us?"

"Don't worry. I'll talk to everyone involved before I'm through." He stepped away and had a conversation with someone over his personal radio, and I had to wonder if the band was being detained even as we tried our best to listen in.

When Kevin Hurley finished up, he turned back to us. "That's taken care of. They'll be held until I have a chance to speak with them."

Maddy pulled out her telephone as Kevin spoke, and he put a hand on hers before she could dial. "Who do you think you're calling?"

"I have to phone Sharon," Maddy said as she tried to pull her phone away.

"Who exactly is Sharon?" Kevin asked.

"She's Grant's mother. Kevin, if you haven't told her yet, I want to break it to the woman myself. She's getting older, and the shock of hearing about what happened to her son just might kill her."

The police chief looked very uncomfortable suddenly, and for some crazy reason, I wasn't all that surprised when he said, "You don't know, do you?"

"Know what?" Maddy asked.

"I didn't realize that the two of you were that close. I'm sorry, Maddy, but Sharon died last week herself."

"Was she murdered, too?" I asked.

"Why would you jump to that particular conclusion?" the chief asked.

"It seems to be happening a lot lately, that's all," I said lamely.

He decided not to comment on that any further. "No, from what I've heard, her death was strictly due to natural causes. Was that why Grant was here? Was he trying to work up the nerve to tell you about what happened to his mother?"

I looked at Maddy, and we had one of those silent conversations we had grown accustomed to over the years. It was something we'd developed as girls, and the two of us could convey more in a few glances than most kids could manage in half an hour of text messages these days. With my expression, I was arguing that she should go into more detail about Grant's averred reason for coming. I insisted, and she finally agreed.

"I've already told you that he wanted me back in his life," Maddy said reluctantly. "At least that was what he claimed when he came by the pizzeria this afternoon. What I didn't tell you about was his level of enthusiasm, and the harshness of my rejection of the very idea of ever being with him again."

"So, even without your current boyfriend, there was no way you were going to take him back?" Kevin asked her.

"Not on your life," my sister said, and she must have realized how bad it sounded. "What I'm saying is that it wasn't exactly an amicable divorce. I caught him cheating, and not even Grant was stupid enough to believe that I would ever take him back after that happened. Honestly, I don't even know why he'd want to try. He had to know what I would say to any attempt he made to reconcile with me."

"My guess is that he had some kind of ulterior motive," I said.

"Hang on a second," the chief said as he looked oddly at me. "There's something in the squad car I want you to look at, Maddy."

He started back to his car, and I saw Maddy put a hand on Bob's as she whispered, "Are you okay?"

"I'm fine. *You're* the one I'm worried about," he said. "I know he wasn't a great guy, but you loved him enough at one point to marry him, and I'm truly sorry for your loss."

Maddy shook her head as she began to cry, and I had to check myself to keep from consoling her myself. Bob was doing a fine job of it, and there was no need for anything but an extra pat on her shoulder from me. David looked like he had no idea what he should be doing, so I smiled at him to try to reassure him.

The chief came back with a letter that had clearly been folded at one time but was now open fully in a plastic evidence bag. There was enough light coming from the porch that Maddy could read it, and I did my best to look over her shoulder so that I could see it for myself.

It was some kind of legal document, and I saw a scrawled signature at the bottom of it. It looked a bit like Maddy's, but not enough to fool me.

"That's a forgery," I said the second I saw it.

"That's what I'm trying to find out," the chief said. "Maddy, *is* that your signature? Did you sign this document today?"

"No, of course not. What is it?"

"It's a quitclaim deed," Bob said, clearly recognizing it for what it was. "It's pretty common in my circles."

"What exactly does it mean, though?" Maddy asked.

Bob looked at the document in question a little closer and then said, "If you *had* signed it, you would have relinquished any and all of your rights to the estate of Sharon Appleton Whitmore."

"But I didn't even know that she was dead," Maddy protested. "Why would my former mother-in-law leave me anything in her will, anyway?"

"That's kind of what I was hoping you'd be able to tell me," Chief Hurley said.

"I wish I knew, but in all honesty, I don't have a clue."

The chief nodded and then said, "Grant's sister, Rebecca, is coming by in the morning to handle things for the family, so if you'd like to ask her, you can."

"Just give me a time and a place and I'll be there," Maddy said. "I still don't understand why Grant would forge my signature in the first place. The second I found out that he'd done it, I would tell everyone that it wasn't mine."

The chief shook his head. "Don't ask me to explain why the man did what he did. I'm just trying to catch his killer."

"Well, I can assure you that none of us did it," Bob said stiffly.

"We'll see," the chief said. "Counselor, you're not planning any trips out of Timber Ridge in the near future, are you?"

"I have a thriving law practice here," Bob answered. "I'm not going anywhere."

"Good," the chief said and then he turned to David. "How about you?"

"I'm supposed to visit a few branches of my company out of town in the next few weeks," he answered.

"Could you put that on hold for now?" Kevin asked him.

"I'll do what I can," David said.

"What about us?" I asked. "Should Maddy and I stick around, too?"

"With you both working at the Slice day and night, I kind of took it for granted that you'd be around if I needed you."

"You don't honestly suspect that Maddy and I could have stabbed Grant together, do you?" I asked.

"I'm not ready to say one way or the other about anything just yet," he said as he moved back to his patrol car. "Have a nice evening, or what's left of it." He paused and then turned to Maddy. "I'm sorry I had to just spring Mrs. Whitmore's death on you like that. It's pretty clear that you cared about her."

"She was a fine woman, and she deserved a better son than she got," Maddy said. "I know I shouldn't speak ill of the dead like that, but Grant wasn't perfect by any stretch of the imagination, and I won't pretend that he was just because he's gone."

After Chief Hurley left, we all stood around in the front yard, the party mood now broken completely.

Maddy finally asked, "Bob, what should we do?"

"For now? Nothing would be the best course of action. None of us killed your ex-husband, and I have faith the police chief will determine that soon enough."

"Then you've got more faith in him than I do," Maddy said.

"Maddy," I said, scolding her softly.

"Let's face it, Eleanor. He can handle bicycle thefts and petty larceny just fine, but when he's investigating murder, it's not too tough for him to get in over his head. We need to figure out who killed Grant ourselves," Maddy said.

"Would it mean anything if I told you that was the *worst* thing that you could do?" Bob asked. "It will just make me look even guiltier than I do now."

"I'm sorry about that, but we can't just stand by and watch the police chief try to hang this on you," Maddy said. "Don't worry. Eleanor and I will be subtle about it."

Bob just shrugged. "I know that you believe you will be."

"That's not exactly a ringing endorsement, is it?" David asked.

I put a hand on his arm. "Bob knows what we've done in the past. He has every right to voice his opinion, since it involves him so directly."

"He told me to hang around town, too, remember? All I'm saying is that if I can help your investigation, all you have to do is ask," David answered.

"As will I," Bob said, and David nodded his approval. "I wasn't doubting your abilities."

"If we need anything, you can believe that we'll ask for it," I said. "In the meantime, there's nothing that any of us can do tonight. Let's just call it a night and tackle everything fresh first thing tomorrow. Maddy, would you like to stay here with me this evening?"

She looked questioningly at Bob, who nodded. He said, "That's most likely for the best. I'm not going to be good company tonight, anyway. You really should stay here with Eleanor."

"That's just a suggestion, though, right?" she asked him with a gentle voice.

"My dear, I'm not foolish enough to try to make it an order," Bob said and then kissed my sister. "Don't worry about me. I'll be fine." He turned to David and then asked, "Shall we get out of here and leave the ladies in peace?"

"That's fine by me," David said and then kissed me good night, a short peck hardly worth the name.

It wasn't until after they were both gone that I realized that Maddy and I were going to have to clean up the mess we'd all made, after all. I almost said something to that effect, trying to get a smile out of her, but I doubted there was much humor that could be salvaged this evening, so I kept it to myself as we cleaned up.

After she was safely in bed, I walked through the house, turning off the lights and checking the locks one final time before I called it a night myself.

I needed my rest if we were going to start our investigation the next day. Though I hadn't lost someone I'd been close to at one time to murder, I had nearly as much motivation to solve Grant's murder as Maddy had. I knew from bitter experience that our lives wouldn't be the same until we could wipe this dark cloud away.

Tomorrow Maddy and I were going to once again go looking for a murderer, and I hoped for all of our sakes that we would be able to find whoever it was who killed Grant Whitmore.

Chapter 4

"Hey, are you awake?" I asked Maddy the next morning as I tapped lightly on the guest-room door.

"Come on in," my sister said, and I pushed the door open to find her sitting up in bed. It was pretty clear by looking into Maddy's eyes that she'd been crying, but I wasn't about to bring it up if she wasn't going to. She had the right to mourn in whatever way she saw fit, and whether it was for Grant or his mother, I was going to respect it.

"How did you sleep?"

"Off and on," she admitted. "You know, I wasn't Grant's biggest fan, but I still can't believe that he's actually dead, can you?"

"I know. It's hard to wrap my head around the

fact that he's gone, too. It would have been one thing if it had happened somewhere else and we hadn't seen him so recently, but this really brought it close to home, didn't it? If I'm being honest about it, he was my least favorite of all your ex-husbands, but that doesn't mean I wanted to see him dead."

Maddy frowned just a little. "Eleanor, there haven't been *that* many husbands," she protested.

I sat down on the edge of her bed. "I know, and I apologize. That was in pretty bad taste, and I shouldn't tease you about it, certainly not right now." It was time to lighten the mood a little. "Are you in the mood for some breakfast?"

"That would be nice," she said. "Any chance you'd make me pancakes?"

"I'm on it," I said as I got up. "You're welcome to take a shower, or even just laze around up here alone if you'd like, but if you're in the mood for some company, I'd be delighted if you'd come into the kitchen while I work."

"I'll be there shortly," she said. "We're still opening today, aren't we?"

"If you're up to it." I'd thought briefly about shutting the Slice down until we found Grant's killer, but there were a few reasons why it wouldn't be such a great idea. I needed the income, since the line between profit and loss was fine indeed, but more importantly, if we shut our presence down to the folks of Timber Ridge, it would most likely look as though we had something to hide. Besides, leaving the pizzeria open might bring us leads or other information that we wouldn't be able to get otherwise. My customers loved to gossip, and with any luck, someone had seen something at the festival last night, and they'd share it with us.

"Eleanor, if it's all the same to you, I need to work, and besides, it might give us a chance to tap into our Timber Ridge network of friends to see if any of our customers saw anything last night that might help us."

"Great minds think alike. I'll see you in a bit."

We were just finishing up with our meal when there was a knock at my door. I approached it tentatively, remembering a few times in the past when the chief of police had come by my place unannounced, either bringing bad news or trying to grill me about something. When I opened the door and saw who it was, though, I started smiling.

"Come on in," I told Bob. "We weren't expecting to see you so early this morning."

"I know. Sorry about that. I should have called first, but I was on my way into my office, and I wanted to have a word with your sister while I had the chance."

As he followed me into the living room, I called out to my sister, "Maddy, Bob's here to see you."

We passed each other as I entered the kitchen. I figured the two of them needed some privacy, and besides, I had dishes to do. I was up to my elbows in soapy water when Maddy came back into the room.

"Did Bob leave already? I didn't even hear the front door close."

"He's surprisingly stealthy, isn't he?" she asked with a smile.

"Is everything all right?"

As Maddy grabbed a towel to dry for me, she said, "I'd be lying if I said that things couldn't be better. Actually, he wanted to know if we were still planning to dig into Grant's murder."

"He's not trying to stop us, is he?" I asked. "You'd think that he'd be all for it, given the situation he's in. Should I talk to him?"

"Hang on a second, Eleanor. Bob just told me that he didn't mean to sound so negative last night about our plans to investigate. He wanted to make sure that I knew that he was all for us seeing what we could find out about Grant, and why anyone would want to kill him."

"Wow, pardon me for saying so, but he was never exactly gung ho about our investigations in the past."

She grinned. "Believe me, I haven't forgotten, either. As a matter of fact, I just reminded him of that."

"What did he say when you did?"

"He told me that after spending a nearly sleepless night, he's come to the conclusion that our digging couldn't hurt, and it might just help. It wasn't exactly high praise, but I took it gladly from him."

"What's he going to do about it himself?" I asked as I finished washing the last plate, rinsed it, and handed it to Maddy to dry.

"He's going to keep a low profile, keep working, and hope that somebody figures out who killed my ex-husband before the rumors and speculation do too much damage to his reputation."

As I drained the water from the sink, I said, "I've been thinking about something, and I was wondering if you had any clue about what Sharon Whitmore might have left you."

Maddy shrugged. "I haven't the slightest idea. We kept in touch after the divorce, but we weren't exactly best friends, if you know what I mean. We spoke on the phone once a month, and a couple of times a year we got together and had lunch."

"How did I not know about that?"

She smiled at me. "Eleanor, I have a life outside of the Slice, even if it's not much of one. As to what she might have left me, I have a hunch it's her slides."

"She had slides? A woman that age? Wasn't she afraid of breaking a hip or something?"

"Photographic slides," Maddy said. "Sharon loved to put on slideshows of her photographs, and I thought they were really quite good, but her own children didn't mask their boredom for her passion."

"What were the pictures of?" I asked.

"Mostly just clouds," Maddy said.

Surely I'd misheard her. "Clowns?" What a garish collection that must be. I'd been distrustful of clowns since my seventh birthday party, when the hired entertainment, a red-nosed mess named Beebobu, showed up drunk and promptly threw up on my Princess Persephone birthday cake.

"Clouds, as in those white puffy things that are up in the sky. She had some remarkable shots, and she was always eager to show me her latest images whenever we got together."

"Why would Grant care if you got those?" I asked.

Maddy shook her head. "It's not all that hard to imagine that he didn't want me to have *anything* of his mother's. Grant didn't make any bones about the fact that he hated that his mother and I still kept in touch. You want to know something? I'm not signing that paper for Rebecca, and I wouldn't have signed it for Grant, either. If Sharon wanted me to have something, then I'm going to make sure I get it. Anything else would dishonor our genuine friendship."

"Clouds," I repeated. "They really must be something."

"Just wait. You'll be impressed. I guarantee it."

"We have some time before we have to go in and prep for opening the Slice today. Who should we speak with first? Do you have any idea where Grant lived?"

"I already tracked it down. I did a little digging last night, after we said good night," she admitted.

"How could you do that? You don't have your computer with you, do you?"

"No, but my phone has Internet access," she admitted. "It's really pretty amazing what I can do with it. You really should upgrade yours, you know."

"No, thanks. I'm not all that keen on having a cell phone at all. The basic unit is just fine for my needs."

She frowned. "Suit yourself. Anyway, I did a few searches on Grant, and believe it or not, I found out that he moved back in with Sharon last year."

"Are you telling me that Grant lived with his mommy?" I asked. It was hard to imagine that self-important and overly inflated ego living under someone else's roof. "What happened to make him do that?"

"He got yet another divorce," Maddy said, "and evidently, the final ex–Mrs. Whitmore had a craftier attorney than I did. She took him to the cleaners but good."

"Could *she* have killed him?" I asked, suddenly very interested in the mystery woman.

Maddy frowned. "I suppose she could have, but why would she? She got three quarters of everything he owned. Why would she want to see him dead, too?"

"That's a question we need to ask her, don't you think? How do we find her?"

Maddy took out her telephone and tapped a few buttons. For all I knew, she was calling up missile launch codes, but after a few seconds, she said, "Her name is Vivian. She lives in Cow Spots, and she owns a dry cleaning business there."

"Did she buy it with her divorce settlement?" I asked.

Maddy tapped a few more keys and then said, "Based on when she bought it, my guess is that she probably did."

"Why a dry cleaner, of all things?" I asked.

"Who knows?" Maddy asked. "So, should we go talk to her before we tackle anyone else?"

"The second you told me that Grant had moved back home, I was hoping that we'd be able to figure out a way to check out Sharon's place first," I admitted.

"Done and done," my sister said with a grin.

"Do you actually have a key?" I asked.

"No, but if things have stayed the same since I was a member of that family, I know where one's hidden. Let's go see what we can find."

"Maddy, are you sure that you're okay with opening the Slice today? If you want to shut it down until we figure out what really happened to Grant, I'm okay with it."

"Last night you were willing to open up today

at our normal time. What changed your mind, Eleanor?"

"I'm still willing to work our normal shift if that's what you want to do, but I don't want to force the decision on you if you think we're killing our time to snoop. Are you honestly okay with us opening today?"

"Are you kidding? I'm counting on it," she said. "We need to make things look like business as usual, you know? Besides, if we don't find any clues on our own, some might just walk in and find us."

"Okay, then we stick to our original plan," I said as I hugged her. "I really am sorry about Grant."

She pulled away and nodded. "Thanks. He was a lousy husband, and not that much better a person overall, but he deserved better than he got. I might be doing this a little because of him, but mostly I'm just trying to protect Bob."

There was one last thing I needed to ask, just to clear the air between us completely. "Maddy, I don't even want to bring this up, but we need to talk about this. Don't get mad, but I have something I need to ask you."

I could see her steel herself for my question. "Go ahead."

"Have you considered the possibility that Bob circled back after we left the fair and killed Grant? If he felt as though the man was a threat to you, he might have acted to protect you from him."

Maddy shrugged. "It crossed my mind for a second when I first heard the news, but I feel pretty secure in my belief that my fiancé didn't do it."

"I know you love him, but we have to keep open minds about this," I said.

"It's not that. I just realized that if Bob wanted to go after someone, he'd find a way to take them to court. I'm pretty sure that's the way he'd punish them."

"I don't know. He was as mad as I'd ever seen him yesterday, Maddy."

She paused a little longer before she answered. "He was defending me, Eleanor. I'm not saying the man is perfect, but he's no killer."

"Not even if he thought you were in real danger?"

She shrugged. "I wish I knew the answer to that, but we aren't going to get anywhere if we start off believing that Bob killed Grant."

"I see what you're saying, but I just wanted to discuss the possibility so we can put it behind us. What are we going to do if we find direct evidence that Bob was the one who killed your ex-husband?"

"We'll turn it over to Chief Hurley, just like we would for anyone else," she said with infinite sadness in her voice. "I'd fight like the devil to get him off, but I won't sweep it under the rug. Can you live with that?"

"I can if you can," I said. I tried to think what I would do if I were in her shoes, with David, or even

Joe, accused of murder. I couldn't honestly answer the question, but I had a new level of respect for my sister. There was no doubt in my mind that she was telling the truth.

I just hoped and prayed that we'd never have to find out what she'd do if the evidence pointed to Bob.

Now, more than ever, it was important that we find the killer, and quickly.

Our plans changed when we got to Sharon's house, though. There were two squad cars parked out front, and I drove on past, hoping that no one would notice us.

"We can always come back later," I said.

"If there's anything left to find," Maddy replied.

"Well, we can't exactly go in right now, can we?"

"Tell you what. We can't afford to waste too much time worrying about this. Let's drive on to Cow Spots, and we can swing back past here when we're finished there. Is that okay with you?"

"It sounds like a plan to me."

"May I help you?" a striking redhead said from behind the counter of the Clean Break Dry Cleaner. She was poured into a tight green dress that showed off every single one of the abundant curves she had, and I wondered how many male customers visited her place just to get a glimpse of her.

"That depends," I said. "Are you Vivian?"

"Who wants to know?" she asked and then spotted Maddy behind me. "Hey. I know you."

"Do you? I'm sorry, but I don't remember meeting you."

"That's because you never did," Vivian said with a smile. "We have something in common, though. We both divorced the same weasel."

It occurred to me that she didn't know that her ex-husband was dead. "I'm afraid we have some bad news for you, if you haven't already heard," I said. "Grant was murdered last night."

"What makes you think that can be viewed as bad news?" she said. This woman was cold. There was no doubt about it. "Anyway, I already heard about it. The cops came by my place at midnight. Fortunately, I had an alibi, so I'm in the clear." She looked at Maddy and asked, "How about you? Are you in hot water over this?"

"No, I have an alibi myself, but my fiancé doesn't," Maddy admitted.

Vivian whistled. "Wow, are you seriously going to get married again after being hitched to Grant? You've got more nerve than I do. I'll give you that. I'm swearing off men myself."

I found that hard to believe, given the way she was dressed, but, hey, it was none of my business, so I kept my mouth shut. "Would you mind telling us what your alibi is?"

She looked at me suspiciously. "I don't see any reason that I should. I don't have to tell you anything."

"Of course you don't," Maddy said. "We're just trying to cross some names off our list of suspects, and we thought you'd be happy to help us, since you have an alibi. It's not going to be easy eliminating the list of suspects we're looking at."

"I don't envy you that," Vivian said.

"So you'll help us?" I asked.

"Not a chance. You can either take my word for it or not. I don't care one way or the other."

"I suppose that we could always ask the police ourselves," I said. I knew there wasn't much chance the police here would be any different from Chief Hurley, but if she thought the threat was more than idle, she might give up the information without me sticking my own neck out.

Her reaction honestly surprised me. Her look was one of defiance as she said, "I wouldn't do that, if I were you."

"Why on earth shouldn't we?" Maddy asked.

"I have friends who wouldn't like it," she said. "Powerful friends."

Was she sleeping with someone in law enforcement, or maybe even in city hall? "We're not afraid of the police, or even the mayor of your little town."

Vivian's laugh was harsh. "You're talking about the wrong side of the law, sweetie. The guys I know don't bother with things like legal or illegal, if you get my meaning."

Was she threatening us with thugs? Little did she know that I had connections on that side of the law as well. "Maybe I can find a way to change your mind," I said.

"I don't think so, but you're welcome to try."

I turned to my sister and said, "Maddy, step outside with me a second, would you?" I didn't want Vivian to hear what I was about to suggest to Maddy.

Vivian looked surprised as I led my sister outside.

Once we were there, I turned to her and said, "Listen, I know you don't like Art Young, and if you don't want me to do this, I won't call him, but he could make things a lot easier for us here right about now."

"Call him," Maddy said.

"Even with your misgivings about my friendship with him?" Maddy hated the fact that Art and I were close. There were rumors and innuendos around Timber Ridge that Art was a Bad Man, but I'd never seen that side of him myself.

"Eleanor, I'm trying to save Bob's reputation here, if not his life. I'd consider it a personal favor if you called Art and asked him for his help."

My sister was more frightened than I'd even imagined if that was the way she truly felt about the situation. "Okay. Give me a second."

I called a number Art had given me once, and

waited for someone to answer. After four rings, a stranger picked up. "I need to speak with Art, please."

"Sorry, but there's nobody named Art here," the man said, and then I remembered that my friend had given me a code to use to get in touch with him. The problem was, I'd completely forgotten what it was.

"Listen, I don't remember if I'm supposed to say, 'The fat man walks alone at midnight' or tell you that birds don't fly upside down, but find him and tell him that Eleanor needs his help and that he can call me on my cell phone."

I hung up, and Maddy looked oddly at me. "I can't believe you did that."

"You just told me that I should call him," I reminded her.

"Not that. It's just that you chewed out someone who might be a very bad man in his own right."

I hadn't even considered that. I was about to answer when my cell phone rang.

After I answered it, Art asked, "Eleanor, are you all right?"

"I am, but I need a favor. But before I forget, could you apologize to the man I just spoke to? I'm sorry about the way I treated him on the telephone."

Art chuckled. "It's not necessary."

"It is to me."

Art paused a moment and then said, "Very well,

but I'm not sure if he's more afraid of you or of me right now. So, what is this favor? Ask, and it's yours."

"Wow, I'm not sure I want a blank check like that. I'm at the Clean Break Dry Cleaner in Cow Spots. A woman named Vivian owns it, and I need her alibi for a murder last night. The only problem is that she won't give it to me, and she claims that she's under someone's protection. Can you help? You know that I wouldn't ordinarily ask, but this is important."

"I assumed that it was about Grant Whitmore when I heard that you had called," he said. "Tell your sister I'm sorry for her loss."

"I will," I said. "Do I even need to ask how *you* heard about it so quickly?"

"Not a great deal goes on in Timber Ridge that I'm not aware of," Art said. "I don't know this Vivian directly. Let me make a few phone calls. How long will you be there?"

"We can wait an hour before we have to leave," I said after glancing at my watch.

"Oh, it won't take that long," he said and then hung up.

"Is he going to help us?" Maddy asked.

"He asked us to wait here. Oh yeah. He also told me to tell you that he was sorry to hear about Grant."

"That's nice of him," Maddy said.

We found a bench near the front of the dry cleaner, in plain view of the picture window, and

Maddy and I waited for Art's return call. Vivian pretended to ignore us, but it was hard to do, since we didn't see a single customer come into the store while we waited. Was the dry cleaner all it seemed to be, or could it be a front for something else? Honestly, I wasn't sure that I wanted to know.

Fourteen minutes after my call to Art, Vivian came out of the dry cleaner and walked toward us. There was a contrite expression on her face, and I didn't have to guess what was motivating her visit to us. Her words just confirmed my suspicion that Art had already acted on our behalf.

"I'm sorry if I was rude before," Vivian said. "I was with a married man named Jack Timbold last night here in town. He'll confirm that we were together if you ask him. Again, I'm sorry for my behavior."

After she went back into her business, my telephone rang. "I trust that was satisfactory," Art said.

"Can we believe her?" I asked.

"There's no doubt in my mind. Lying is not something she would even consider, given the circumstances."

"Then it's perfect. Thank you for acting so quickly. I'm really sorry to bother you with this."

"Eleanor, I am so deeply in your debt that there's nothing you can't ask of me."

I didn't have a chance to respond to that before he hung up.

"So, do we believe her?" Maddy asked.

"I'm inclined to, unless we learn something

otherwise. I have a feeling that Vivian would have a lot more of a problem lying to us, with Art backing us, than she ever would to the police. For now, we can mark her name off our list."

"Our list of suspects is looking kind of sparse at the moment, isn't it?" Maddy asked as we headed to my car.

"I don't know. There's the man from Grant's mysterious meeting we saw last night, and don't forget the lead singer and the guitar player from the band. Who knows how many other folks we'll be able to dig up once we get into this case a little further?"

"I'll be happy just as long as Bob isn't the last name on our list when this is all over," Maddy said.

I wasn't about to admit it, but I was wishing the exact same thing.

"I'd still like to talk to Jack Timbold just to confirm Vivian's alibi," I said.

"Why? I thought we agreed that Vivian wouldn't lie to us, knowing that Art was on our side."

"I'm sure that someone put the fear of Art into her, but what if she did kill Grant and then tried to give herself a false alibi to the police without talking it over with anyone else? I don't doubt that she was with this Timbold guy, but I need to hear it directly from him and find out the exact time they were together. We can't forget that Cow Spots is only twenty minutes from Timber Ridge. She might have set this poor guy up as an alibi after she killed Grant to give herself some cover, never realizing that she might be digging a deeper hole for herself by doing it."

"Okay, then we'll keep him on our list of folks we need to talk to, and Vivian moves to the back burner for now until we do." As I drove back toward Timber Ridge, she asked, "Do we still have time to go by Sharon's and snoop around a little?"

"If the police are finished there, we'll make the time," I said.

"Thanks, Eleanor. I know you don't really have a dog in this fight. I appreciate you committing yourself to the investigation like this."

"Hang on a second," I said to her. "You need to understand something. Bob might be your fiancé, but he's my friend, too, and I never let my friends down. I'm almost as eager as you are to solve this case."

"I'm glad you said *almost*," Maddy answered.

"Is it going to be tough on you being around Sharon's things so soon after learning that she is dead?" I asked her as we now headed toward a stop at her former mother-in-law's address before we made it back to the pizzeria. "I know you cared about her."

"I can't say that I'm looking forward to it, but what choice do I have?"

"I could go inside alone, and you could wait in the car and keep a lookout for me," I suggested.

"Do you honestly think for one second that I could ever do that?" Maddy asked me.

"No. I realize that's never going to happen, but I kind of felt obligated to make the offer, anyway."

"Don't worry about me, Sis. In a very real way, I lost Sharon the moment I found out that her son had cheated on me. We kept our friendship alive, but there was always that unspoken tension between us, no matter how hard we tried to ignore it."

"I understand," I said. Joe's parents had been dead long before we met, and I'd never had the opportunity of having a mother-in-law, good or bad. Sometimes I wondered what I'd missed out on, but mostly, I didn't think about it. It was tough to mourn something that I'd never experienced.

We got to Sharon's house, and thankfully, the police cruisers were gone.

I didn't stop in, though.

"Where are you going, Eleanor?"

"Think about it, Maddy. What if someone comes by while we're in there snooping? Even if they don't, do we really want to advertise the fact to the world that we're digging around here? I figured that it might be prudent to park down the block a little, in case we need to make a quick escape."

"Okay, I can see how that might be a good thing."

After I parked, we walked back toward the house like we had every right in the world to be there.

I just hoped that we could get in.

THE MISSING DOUGH

If the spare key was still where my sister remembered it had been hidden, Maddy and I were about to do some serious snooping into Grant's life.

I just hoped we'd be able to find something that would help.

Chapter 5

"Let's get in before anyone sees us," Maddy said softly as she opened the front door and stepped quickly inside. Just as she had suspected, the key had been buried in the third window box on the right, and she'd pulled it out of the topsoil and flowers as though she used it all the time.

"Lead the way," I whispered as she closed the door behind me.

"Why are you whispering?" she asked in her normal voice.

"Was I?" I asked, but I knew all too well why I'd lowered my voice upon crossing the threshold.

There was something eerie about a house when its owner had recently died. Some folks believed that it was a lingering spirit, and though I couldn't say for sure what I believed one way or the other, I knew that there could often be a presence felt in a place, almost as though something was holding on to a spot where it didn't belong anymore. I would love to be able to say that I'd never personally been in the home of someone who had recently died, but unfortunately, I couldn't make that claim. During past investigations, Maddy and I had searched quite a few houses, looking for clues about who might have wanted to kill their former owners, and the range of experiences we'd had did nothing to discourage that belief.

This was a first, though.

Sharon had passed away recently—peacefully, according to the reports we'd heard—but Grant had been another case entirely. Was it a mixed set of emotions we were going to experience here?

"Has much changed since you were here the last time?" I asked Maddy as I looked around. The house was decorated in a way that clearly was not to my own minimalist taste, with flowery wallpaper adorning the walls, shelves everywhere covered with teacups of all shapes and sizes, and furniture that looked as though it'd been there for several decades. For a moment I could almost taste the feeling of loss all around us. Man, oh, man, my imagination was running away with me. If I was being honest about it, there was little doubt in my mind that I was just creating these impressions myself, but that didn't make them any easier to take.

"Should we search the upstairs?" I asked, hoping that the space had to be less stressful than where we were standing at the moment.

"It's my best guess about where we'll find Grant's room," she agreed.

The odd thing was that there was no evidence that he'd been living in the house at all. We checked every bedroom and the hall bathroom upstairs as well, but I didn't see a single sign that Grant had been there in the past ten years. Even his boyhood bedroom was covered with a fine layer of dust. "Maddy, I don't know about you, but I don't think Grant ever lived here after the two of you were married. Could your source on the Internet have been wrong?"

She frowned. "I'm not willing to give up yet. We still need to check the basement."

"Would she make him live down there when all of these bedrooms are empty upstairs?" I asked.

"If he stayed there, it was most likely Grant's choice," Maddy said. "If he was living in the basement, he could delude himself into believing that he had a place of his own. I'm not sure he could live with the idea that he had to come home and live with his mother again. Come on. Let's check it out."

Maddy opened the basement door, and as she did, I could swear I felt a fleeting, cold burst of air escape. The impression lasted just an instant, but it felt real just the same. It was as though the upstairs was filled with Sharon's spirit, while Grant's ghost had stayed in the basement, where it belonged.

"I'm seriously losing my mind with all of this," I said aloud, trying to break the spell this house seemed to hold over me.

"I don't doubt it for one second, but why now in particular?" Maddy asked as we walked down the steps together.

"This place feels as though it's haunted by two different ghosts," I admitted to my sister. "Upstairs was warm and open, but this is downright hostile."

Maddy chuckled a little. "Sharon was always complaining that the basement was a little drafty. As for the upstairs, it's *always* been too warm for my taste."

"So, you think I'm just imagining it?"

"I wouldn't say that. Who knows what happens after we're gone? Maybe neither one of them was ready to walk into the light."

We were at the bottom of the stairs, and I had to look hard at the expression on Maddy's face to see if she was making fun of me. There was no sign of amusement there, though, something that didn't really comfort me.

I probably would have liked it better if I knew that she'd been teasing me.

Maddy flipped a light switch, and I could see that the downstairs was indeed some kind of subterranean apartment. It had been decorated sometime in the seventies, and no one had updated it since. The walls were painted a mustard brown, and the carpet was a lighter shade of yellow. It wouldn't have surprised me to find black lights and disco balls hanging from the ceiling, but fortunately, we were spared that. Still, it was no place for a grown man to be living.

"Vivian must have wiped him completely out to force him to live down here for one day," Maddy said.

"After meeting her, can you honestly say that it surprises you? She had that kind of look about her, don't you think?"

"I wouldn't trust her to hold on to my lunch money," Maddy admitted. "What I want to know is how Grant ever persuaded her to marry him in the first place."

"I've got a feeling that it was more Vivian's idea than Grant's. She must have had her reasons, but I can't even begin to guess what they could have been."

Maddy looked around the space and then noted, "At least there's not much we have to search."

"And I don't doubt that it's even less after the police left," I said. "Still, we've found things before that they've missed. Kevin Hurley is a pretty good cop, but he lacks something we have when it comes to digging."

"What's that?" Maddy asked.

"A woman's point of view," I answered. "We can see things that he might miss, and better yet, interpret them in a different light."

"I just hope we find something," Maddy said.

I looked around the room and made an executive decision. "Tell you what. You take the closet, and I'll take the desk in the corner. The first one who finishes gets to tackle the chest of drawers."

"It's a deal," she said. As my sister looked into the jammed closet, she said, "I'll never find anything digging around in here. I'm going to search everything as I pull it out of the closet. Do you mind if I use the bed?"

"Be my guest," I said.

As Maddy started investigating the closet, I moved to Grant's desk. It was an old-fashioned rolltop number with dull brass knobs and a well-worn top, and there was no doubt in my mind that it was left over from generations past, just waiting to be put back into use.

At least I didn't need a key. The police who'd searched the place earlier hadn't found it either, but they hadn't let that stop them. There were fresh scratches by the latch, as though someone had pried the tambour pull-down free from its simple lock. It was a rather inelegant way to handle the situation, but I knew that sometimes cops didn't care, especially if they were in a hurry. I shoved the tambour up, hearing it *click, click, click* as it moved up into the desk, to reveal a dozen tiny little drawers and just as many open cubbyholes.

It was time to start digging.

"Did you find anything good yet?" Maddy asked as she walked over to me. I was trying to study Grant's receipts that I'd pulled from the main drawer, searching in vain to find any particular order to his organization, or lack thereof. If it was present, it had eluded me so far. I had moved a few things from the mess over to one side to study later, but I hadn't found anything earth-shattering so far.

I pushed away from the desk. "Was he always such a bad record keeper?"

"Oh, yes. When we first got married, I had to put some extra money in his checking account to cover his rounding habits, and then I had to open a whole new account at another bank so we could start off together with some semblance of organization. It drove me mad."

"I can't even imagine how you were able to stand it," I said. "How about you? Were you able to find anything?"

She didn't look particularly happy as she admitted, "I'm just about all the way to the back of the closet, and so far, I've pulled four notes from his pockets. Two were written on napkins, one on a pack of matches, and the last one on an old envelope."

"Anything there that you think might be significant?"

She shook her head. "Not that I can tell so far. Three look like telephone numbers, and the final one appears to be some kind of combination."

"He actually has a *safe*?" I asked as I looked around the room for where it might be hiding.

"Not as far as I can see," she said. "What about you?"

I pointed to the small stack of papers I had accumulated so far. "I have no idea what I've got here. I wish we could find his checkbook. The register might be informative."

"The police probably took it with them," Maddy said. "Is his address book anywhere in sight?"

"I didn't know he had one. If it's here, I haven't come across it yet. What does it look like?"

"If you can believe it, it's actually one of those little black books. He keeps everything in it, not just telephone numbers, so if we can track it down, it's going to be a big help."

"I'll keep digging," I said.

"So will I," she said.

Three minutes later Maddy said, "Bingo!"

I left the desk and hurried to the closet. "What did you find? Did the little black book turn up?"

"No, I wasn't that lucky, but I did find five hundred dollars in an envelope tucked in the pocket of his best suit."

"We aren't here scavenging for cash, Maddy."

She shook her head. "I'm just saying, this must mean something. Grant was notorious for putting everything on his credit card. Why would he be carrying around a wad of cash like this?"

"I don't have a clue, but you should put it back where you found it."

"Eleanor, I know that we can't keep it, but couldn't we use it for expenses while we're digging into his murder?"

"I suppose that's one way to look at it," I said. "But I still don't think that I could feel right about doing it. As far as I'm concerned, it should go into the estate. Who knows? Maybe you'll get a bit of it for yourself."

"I'm not counting on it," she said with a wry smile as she laid the envelope on top of the desk. "I'll be amazed if I get anything better than Sharon's slides, and maybe that teacup collection we saw on the way in."

"You never know," I said.

I tried to pull out the last and biggest lower drawer in the desk, and when it wouldn't budge, I saw that it was locked. There were more fresh scratch marks on the wood, and after fiddling with it a little, I was able to open it.

Whatever had been there when the police had started their search was now gone. I stared at the bottom of the drawer for a minute, though. Something was wrong. It took a little time, but then I got it. The bottom of the drawer should have been deeper than it was. Not by much, but enough to allow a few things to be hidden there. Once I pulled it all the way out, I searched the back of the drawer with my fingers and felt a small wire button hidden there. As I pressed it, the wooden bottom shifted upward, releasing some kind of catch inside the drawer. Lifting the false bottom out, I eagerly looked inside the drawer to see what had been hidden away. I had a hunch that the police had missed this in their search.

Inside, there were two stacks of hundred-dollar bills, and I quickly counted them as I removed them. One stack had five thousand dollars in it, and the other was five hundred short of that total. It appeared that I'd found a secret money stash, but that wasn't what interested me the most. The drawer also had a handful of letters in it, carefully banded together, as well.

I was about to pick them up when I heard someone fumbling with a key in the lock upstairs.

Someone was trying to get in!

It was clear by the false starts that they were having trouble finding the right key, but I suspected it was just a matter of seconds before we had company.

"Maddy, we need to get out of here. Is there a back way out of here?"

"There's a door to the outside, but why should we leave?"

She'd had her head buried in the closet, so she

must not have heard the first few keys in the lock. At that moment, there was another false start, and she scooped up her pile of finds, along with a few other things, and headed for the door. "Come on. Let's go. There's a basement access door over this way," she said.

I considered taking the money for one brief second, but on second thought, I grabbed the letters instead, as well as the documents I'd gathered myself. Taking more time than I really had, I jammed the cash, including the five hundred bucks Maddy had found, into the drawer and put the false bottom in place. Upstairs, it sounded as though whoever was trying to get in was getting closer. There was a loud click as the right key hit home, and I hurried to catch up with Maddy.

She was standing by the basement door, waving me on. "Hurry up," she whispered.

I raced for the back door as I heard footsteps upstairs, and I was sorry that I hadn't at least closed the door from the first floor to the basement. As the footsteps neared, I nearly dove out the basement door, and Maddy eased it shut just as we heard someone on the steps coming down to where we'd just been.

"They're going to see the mess we left," Maddy said as we hurried away.

"We can't do anything about that now. Maybe they'll think the cops did it. Nobody's going to suspect us."

THE MISSING DOUGH

As we hurried around the house and down the street, Maddy finally eased her pace and said, "That was good thinking, parking away from the place."

"Thanks. I get a good idea every now and then," I said as I glanced at my watch. "We need to get to the Slice. I still have time to make fresh dough, so we don't have to rely on our frozen stash. We can look at what we managed to get out of there after we finish our prep work for the day."

"Or I could start digging into it right now while you drive us to Timber Ridge," Maddy suggested.

There was no way that I could make her wait, nor did I really want to. "Go on, then. Let's see what we were able to come up with."

As she looked through the stack of papers we'd retrieved, she said, "You left the money, I see."

"I told you I was going to," I said.

I was about to tell her about the other cash I had found when she added, "How much do you want to bet that dear, sweet Rebecca takes it all and fails to disclose it to anyone else?"

"That might be kind of hard for her to do," I said with a grin.

"Why's that?"

I told her about the other cash I'd found and what I'd done with it, all on a whim.

Maddy laughed as she applauded. "That's brilliant. What do you suppose was valuable enough to hide with the cash?"

"I don't know. I never really got the chance to check it out, but it's sitting right there in your lap."

"Then let's check it out right now."

Maddy took off the bands holding the letters in place and then started going through them.

"Hey, the least you could do is read them aloud as you go through them."

"Sorry. I got caught up in what I was doing." She started flipping through the letters and then looked up at me. "I don't get it. Eleanor, they aren't anything."

"What do you mean?"

"Apparently, he really *was* fond of Vivian. These are all letters she wrote him over the past year."

I shook my head. "Seriously? That's kind of odd, isn't it? Grant never struck me as being all that sentimental when the two of you were together."

"He could be when he wanted to be," she said. "Not that he kept any letters I ever wrote him, I'm sure."

"In all fairness, did you ever write him any?" I asked.

She laughed slightly. "Now that you mention it, not that I can remember. I did leave him a few notes over the years, but there wasn't anything newsworthy in any of them."

"So the hidden drawer was a bust," I said.

"I wouldn't say that. There's ten grand still in there. I wouldn't exactly call that a dead end."

"Maybe not, but why would he keep that kind of cash on hand, especially if Vivian had drained him?"

"I can think of some reasons," Maddy said. "He could have been hiding it from her, paying off a debt, or maybe he just won a bet. Then again, he might have planned on using it to get out of town in a hurry."

"Why would he do that?" Maddy was my expert on the topic of her ex, so I had to rely on her gut feeling about Grant's reasoning for doing anything.

"He was always up to something shady," she said. "Who knows? Maybe he was blackmailing somebody, and that was his ill-gotten gains."

"If that's true, where's the evidence he was holding over them? It's got to be there somewhere, too."

"Maybe they paid him off, he gave the evidence back, and the victim stabbed him and tried to retrieve the money, too."

"Hang on. That sounds kind of like a leap to me. Has he ever done anything like that before that you know of?"

"I had my suspicions, but I could never prove anything. Grant liked to keep things close to the vest, but he did act oddly from time to time. We'd be broke one minute, and then the next we'd be flush, with absolutely no explanation from him about what had changed things. Add to it a few whispered conversations I caught him having just before we had money again, and it all makes sense."

"Okay, we'll keep that possibility in mind," I said.

We were nearly back in Timber Ridge when my sister said, "Wow. Will you look at this."

"I'm trying to, but I can't tell what it is from the way you're holding it," I said.

"Sorry. Pull over for one second."

"We're going to be late if we take any breaks," I explained.

"It's worth it. Trust me on that."

I did as she asked, and once I was safely parked on the side of the road, Maddy handed something to me.

"What's this supposed to be?" I asked as I opened the envelope she'd given me and studied what was there. I found just one thing; there was a laundry ticket inside, and the name printed on it was Clean Break.

Did it mean that Grant had clothes ready to be picked up at Vivian's cleaning store, or was there another, darker reason he'd tucked it into an envelope?

"You know, there's a chance that this might not mean anything at all," I said as I put the ticket back in its place.

"Or it could be something really important," Maddy said. "Did you see what was written on the envelope?"

I hadn't, so I turned it over and saw that there was an odd series of numbers written on it. There were too many digits, and they were not spaced properly for it to be a telephone number. "What does it mean?"

"I don't know, but I don't think there's a chance it's just innocent dry cleaning, do you?"

"We'll look into it, I promise," I said as I started driving again.

We were almost at the Slice, and I was suddenly in a hurry to get back to my safe haven, the pizzeria. It was a refuge for me, something Joe and I had created out of our sweat and tears. Though Maddy and I often discussed murder there, the place still managed to hold me in its warmth, as the joyous memories I'd had there far outweighed everything else.

We pulled up in back of the Slice, and Maddy grabbed our finds as we got out of the car. We walked through the shortcut, and I glanced over at the mural painted there. Timber Ridge had done all in its power to draw folks to the promenade, and as a business owner there, I was mighty grateful for all they'd done. We were through the passageway and on our way to the blue section of buildings where the Slice was when I heard a pounding on a window nearby. Paul, our dear friend and the best baker in our part of North Carolina, was waving frantically to us from inside his shop.

"What do you suppose is going on with him?" I asked Maddy as we hurried to meet him at his front door.

"I don't know, but I've got a hunch that we're about to find out."

Chapter 6

"Paul, what's wrong?" I asked when he met us outside.

"I'm so glad that I caught you. Somebody came by here looking for you not too long ago, and I wanted to give you a heads-up before you got to the Slice," he said.

"Was it Rebecca Whitmore?" Maddy asked.

"I don't know who that is, but no, it wasn't her," Paul said.

He was about to continue when Maddy interrupted. "Believe me, you can't miss her if you ever see her. She's slim, nearly six feet tall, kind of pretty, if you like that type, and the last time I saw her, she had long brown hair."

"No, I haven't seen her," Paul said. "I'm talking about Art Young."

"Art came by?" I asked, more startled than I meant to show. "Did he say what he wanted?"

"He didn't tell me anything about why he was hunting for you. He just asked me to tell you when I saw you that the two of you need to talk, and he left this envelope for me to give to you in case I ran into you first. He was pretty insistent about it."

I took the envelope from Paul as he added, "Eleanor, I know that you two are acquaintances, but that doesn't mean you don't need to watch your step around him. From what I've heard, he's connected. Listen, if you need a little cash to get through a rough spot, I'd be glad to loan you everything that's in my account, and it's interest free."

I had to laugh. "Art is more than a passing acquaintance to me. He's my friend, Paul." I waved the envelope in the air. "There's no way this has cash in it. I'm curious, though. Why do you think I might need money?"

He just shrugged. "Hey, don't forget I run a small business, too. I know how tight things can get sometimes." He took a step backward as he added, "I didn't mean to overstep my bounds. You and Maddy are two of the best friends I have in Timber Ridge. I can't help it if I'm a little over-protective of you both."

Maddy and I laughed, and we each found one of his cheeks to kiss. Paul smiled, but it was clear he wasn't all that comfortable with our public display of affection. That was just too bad, though. He was like a part of our family, a big brother who just happened to be younger than either one of us. That didn't mean that he still couldn't look out for the two of us, though.

"Just for the record," I said, "we're fine, financially and otherwise. I have no idea what's in this envelope, but it has nothing to do with money, I can guarantee that to you. By the way, how's your love life these days?"

Paul managed to look uncomfortable yet again. I knew that he was still seeing Gina Sizemore, the young woman who ran Tree-Line. It was an elegant resort hotel and conference center on the edge of town, and they were still dating, at least as of the festival last night. I'd seen them together there, walking around the promenade, holding hands and looking as though the rest of the world wasn't even there. "It's fine," he said.

"Oh, it's bound to be better than just fine," Maddy said with a wicked gleam in her eye. "We've seen the two of you in public."

His face was beginning to turn crimson red. "Maddy, let's stop picking on him," I said as I waved the envelope in the air. "Thanks for delivering this, Paul."

"I was happy to do it," he said.

"Even with Art's reputation around town?" I asked.

"Hey, any friend of yours is a friend of mine," he said.

I had the envelope open by the time my sister and I got to the Slice's front door.

"What does it say?" Maddy asked.

"Hang on a second. We can look at it once we're inside."

I let us into the pizzeria and then locked the door behind us once we were inside. I looked in the envelope, honestly not sure what I was going to find.

There was a single business card in there, with no name and no other indication of who it might belong to. On the front was a telephone number, and on the back, in block letters, someone had printed *Call me ASAP.*

I showed it to Maddy.

"That's odd," she said after she studied it for a few seconds. "I wonder what this is all about."

"There's only one way to find out," I said.

I grabbed my cell phone and dialed the number on the card.

It took twelve rings for whoever was on the other end to answer.

"I'll be outside in seven minutes," Art said and then hung up.

I was still frowning at the phone in my hand when Maddy asked, "What did he say?"

"Art wants to see me. He's coming by soon, but I still think I have time to mix the dough, if you'll help me."

"You shouldn't make him wait, Eleanor," Maddy said.

"He'll understand," I said, hoping that he would. Art knew how much my restaurant meant to me, and even if I was a minute or two late, I was pretty sure that he'd forgive me.

"I hope you're right, but we'd still better get on it," Maddy said.

We measured out flour, yeast, sugar, salt, and water and got the large mixer started.

I handed a spatula to Maddy. "Stop it in two minutes and scrape the sides, okay?"

"I've done this a few times myself," Maddy reminded me. "Go on. You're going to be late."

I took my apron off and grabbed my light jacket on the way out the door.

Art's car was already parked in the promenade parking lot.

It appeared that I hadn't made my deadline, after all.

"I'm sorry I'm late," I said as Art's chauffeur held the door open for me. "Did you have to wait long?"

"Not enough to matter," Art said.

After I slid in beside him, the chauffeur closed the door, and soon after, the car started moving.

"I hate to tell you this, but I really don't have time to go anywhere right now," I said.

"This is important," Art said. "I wouldn't ask if it weren't."

"Okay, I get that. You've got my attention. Let me call Maddy and tell her that I'm not sure when I'll be back."

Art put a hand on mine. He was a man of slight stature, and his carefully styled blond hair was beginning to thin, but there was an air of importance to him that was undeniable. "There's no need for that. We won't be that long."

I shrugged and moved my hand away from the phone. "Okay, if your goal was to intrigue me, you've certainly managed it. What's going on?"

He took a deep breath, as if buying time to word his next statement carefully. "The inquiry I made this morning about the dry cleaner has aroused more interest than it should have. I asked a favor from a friend, but apparently, it was noticed by others."

"That doesn't sound good," I said. "I'm sorry if I got you into trouble."

He shook his head. "Whatever is happening right now has been brewing for some time," he explained. "I'm afraid that this was just the catalyst that is bringing things to a head. I have to ask you not to approach the woman who runs the cleaner again until you've heard directly from me. Will you promise me that you'll do that, Eleanor?"

What was going on with him? I didn't think Art was afraid of anyone or anything, but I was getting some odd vibes from him at the moment. "Art, are you okay?"

"I'm fine, Eleanor. It's *you* I'm concerned about, though. Will you do as I ask? It's important, to both of us."

"I need to talk to her again sometime. Vivian told me her alibi, but I still have a hard time believing it." I took a deep breath and then decided to tell him what I'd found at Grant's basement apartment. "I found an envelope with a string of numbers written on it in Grant Whitmore's desk. Inside the envelope, there was a stub from Clean Break. Does this have anything to do with what's going on?"

"I'm not sure yet, but to be safe, you need to forget about it, at least for the moment. Eleanor, there are some elements that might try to use my friends against me, and you're high up on their list."

"Me?" I asked, shocked by the idea. "Why would anyone feel threatened by me?"

"I'm afraid that our relationship has been noticed in particular circles. For the time being, we can't be seen together, and I'm not at all sure that it's safe for us to communicate in any way. We are going to have an apparent rift in our friendship, at least as far as the world is concerned. It pains me to do this, but it's a necessary step for your safety."

"You're not trying to ditch me, are you?" I asked. "I have plenty of friends, but I'm not in the mood to lose any of them, especially you."

"Your loyalty is without reproach," he said. "This is just something that we have to do. Maddy cannot know, nor your boyfriend or her fiancé. It must be a complete break if it's going to work at all. Will you do this, no matter how distasteful it seems, as a favor to me?"

"Fine, but you should know something. I care more about you than this murder investigation. If I'd had any idea I was getting you in hot water, I never would have asked for your help."

"You can always feel free to request whatever you need from me," Art said. "I'm just not certain that I can always acquiesce."

"Got it." I noticed that we were back in front of the Slice, and I started to get out. "Call me as soon as you can," I said.

"Good-bye, Eleanor," he said, and his driver quickly drove away.

I walked back into the Slice and realized that I could find a way to tell Maddy what was happening without coming right out and saying it definitively. Art's tone had spooked me, and I wasn't afraid to admit it, even if it was only to myself.

"What did he have to say?" Maddy asked me the second I neared the door. "Did he have another clue for us about Vivian?"

"We're not going to see each other anymore," I said. The sadness I felt as I said it, even if it was only temporary, was real enough. Art Young and I didn't exactly have any standing times or dates when we got together, and I never knew *when* I was going to see him, but knowing for sure that I wasn't going to talk to him for the foreseeable future was pretty unpleasant.

"What happened?" Maddy asked, the concern clear in her voice.

"I can't talk about it," I replied, which was true enough. "Apparently, Vivian has something to do with it, and Art warned me that approaching her again anytime soon would be dangerous."

"Dangerous? Seriously?"

"If you'd heard his warning, you wouldn't doubt it for one second."

"So, what do we do?" Maddy asked. "She's not in the clear, by any means. I don't care if the police believe her or not."

"For now, we put her on the back burner," I said. "We've got plenty of other folks to investigate at the moment."

"Like who?" Maddy asked.

"Well, we can track down that man Grant was talking to in the shadows last night, and we can also find out where the people in that band live. That gives us three right off the bat, and who knows where all of that might lead?"

"I don't like this," Maddy said.

"Which part of it? The fact that we have only three suspects, or that somebody might be coming after us because of what we've done?"

"None of that, actually. We both know that we've started with less in the past, and threats have never bothered us," she said. "I just can't imagine Art

Young dumping you like that. You've stood by him in the past when everyone else in town thought you were crazy. It just doesn't make sense."

"Maddy, I've told you all that I can right now. Let's just drop it, okay?"

"Sure, Sis. That's fine with me, if it's what you really want."

"It is," I said, thinking about how stern Art had been when we'd spoken. "What do you say we finish our pizza prep for the day and get on with our lives?"

"That sounds good to me," she said. "What about the rest of the things we found at Grant's, though? We're still going to dig into those, aren't we?"

"You bet we are," I said. "I'm more determined than ever to find out who killed your ex-husband, no matter what it takes."

After the dough was finished and put in the fridge, Maddy had the veggies and meat chopped up for the day's customers. I was cleaning off the counter when Maddy brought out the papers we'd removed from Grant's place.

"Where should I spread these out?" she asked.

"Bring that card table out from my office," I suggested. "It should be big enough for what we need, and I don't really like working at our prep station."

"I can do that," she said. "Here. Hold these while I go grab it."

She shoved the papers into my hands and got

the table out from storage. There was just enough room for it in our kitchen, and after she was finished setting the table up, I handed her half the stack as I glanced at the clock.

"Okay, we've got less than twenty minutes, so we'll have to do a quick sort first," I said.

"I'm fine with that. Let's put the useless stuff in a pile over here, and we'll keep the goodies here. Let's get started."

The first things I pulled out of my pile were the phone numbers she'd retrieved from the clothes hanging in the closet. "Should we just call these and see who answers?"

"We could, but then they'll know what we're up to. Let me call Josh first. I've got an idea."

Josh Hurley was one of our employees and the chief of police's son. I knew that his family wasn't all that thrilled with him working at the Slice for a host of reasons, but I was glad to have him on my staff. He was working part-time during his first year of college, while my other part-timer was Greg Hatcher. He worked at the Slice as well, but he didn't have to. In fact, he had more money than I did, but he loved the place almost as much as Maddy and I did, and we were both grateful to have him. Josh was our resident computer guy these days, and he rarely showed up for his shifts without some kind of computer in his backpack.

"Why don't I call him," I said as Maddy started to dial his number.

"That's fine with me," she said as she put her

phone away. "You do that, and I'll keep digging." Ordinarily, I knew that she wouldn't give in that easily, but there were other things to examine, and my sister's sense of curiosity was probably as bad as mine.

"Josh, it's Eleanor," I said after he picked up.

"Hey, Eleanor," he answered sleepily. "Was I supposed to work the lunch shift today? I must have slept in."

"No, you aren't scheduled until tonight. I need a favor, though."

"Anything for you," he said, coming more and more awake.

"I need you to check out some telephone numbers for me with that magic computer of yours."

"I keep telling you, it's not the computer. It's the user."

"Fine. Have it your way. Are you ready?"

"Give me one second. I need to turn everything on first." As we waited, he asked, "What's this about, anyway?"

"I'm just trying to track some things down," I said. I wasn't being vague because Kevin was his father. I hated dragging the two guys I worked with into my investigations. Sometimes it couldn't be helped, but I never used them unless I had no other choice.

"Gotcha. Mind my own business," he said with a goofy little laugh.

"That's about it," I said, smiling in return, though he couldn't see it.

"Okay, fire away."

"Let's do these one at a time."

I gave him the first number on the matchbook, and a few seconds later, he said, "That's Beth Anne Osler. She lives at Two-Thirty-One West Avenue in Higgins Bottom. Do you need more info about her? I can do a search in no time at all."

"I'm not sure exactly how much detail I need," I said.

"Here it is, anyway. Man, this chick should learn how to set the privacy settings on Facebook. She looks like a real party girl, and when she's not carousing around, she works at the power company in the collections department."

"That's great," I said as I put the matchbook aside.

"I don't know. It's kind of a crazy lifestyle, if you ask me. You should see some of the pictures she has posted on her cube. Should I forward them to you?"

"No thanks. That won't be necessary."

"Okay, who's next on your list?" he asked.

We quickly determined that the next two numbers belonged to women who were just as vapid as Beth Anne appeared to be, and when I got to the last one, I was expecting more of the same.

"Eleanor, this is a dude," he said after he tracked down the number.

"What's his name?"

"Bernie Maine. It looks like a new number, too. How is this guy even a part of something that has those three women in it? Forget it. Don't answer that. I don't want to get you into trouble with my dad."

"What can you tell me about Bernie?"

"This one's going to be a little harder," he said. "There's no Facebook page, and it looks like old Bernie likes to keep his secrets."

"It's okay if you can't find anything," I said.

"Hey, slow down, Boss. I didn't say that I couldn't do it. It's just going to take a minute or two longer, that's all." As he typed more on his keyboard, he began to read the information out loud as he found it. Josh was so involved in what he was doing that I doubted he even realized that he was doing it. "He owns at least two businesses. There's no love life to speak of that I can see. Okay, here's something new. He just shut one of his businesses down completely."

"Can you tell me more about that one?"

"You've got it." Twenty seconds later he said, "It was called Orion Enterprises. They speculated in land development, but it looks like they never were very successful at it. It doesn't surprise me. In my management class, the prof told us that ninety percent of all small businesses fail in the first year. This one looked doomed from the start."

"How can you possibly know that?" I asked, marveling at just how much information was out there about all of us if you had a wizard like Josh searching. Was there any real privacy anymore?

"A quick glance at the company info practically shouts it."

"Do you know who else might have been involved with the organization?"

"Sure. There's a list right here. Besides Bernie, there were two other partners. One was Samantha Stout, and the other was Grant Whitmore. Hey, he's the guy that got murdered last night! How's Maddy taking it?"

"She'd be better if folks didn't suspect Bob was behind the killing," I said.

"Yeah, that really bites. Anyway, is there anything else I can do for you?"

"One more thing. Can you give me addresses and any other viable telephone numbers you can find for Bernie Maine and Samantha Stout?"

"Will do." Less than a minute later I disconnected the call, with the requested information scribbled down on an old menu.

"Wow, that was quite a conversation you just had," Maddy said. "Maybe I shouldn't have given in so easily. I had time to go through everything else while you were chatting with Josh. What all did he say?"

After I brought her up to date on our conversation, I asked Maddy, "What did you uncover?"

"Not much," she admitted. "Did you say that woman investor's name was Samantha Stout, Eleanor?"

"I did."

"I saw her name somewhere else this morning," Maddy said.

"Do you remember where?"

She searched through one of the piles and pulled out a business card with a musical note on it. "Here it is. Southern Sky is the name of the group last night. Grant had one of their cards in his pocket. The members are listed on the bottom edge, and one of them is the lady in question. Funny, but so is one of the guys."

"He's named Samantha Stout, too?"

"Don't be silly. Kenny Stout is listed, though, so I'm betting that he's either her brother or her husband."

"Can I see that?" I asked.

Maddy handed it over, and I flipped to the back. There was nothing but a heart drawn there. That had to mean that Grant was not only an investor with her but probably something else, as well. "I know that Grant cheated on you, but would he do it with a married woman?"

"I don't think he ever let the marital status of anyone involved bother him," she said. "Why do you ask?"

"I'm just trying to figure something out here. I need to call Josh back."

"Wow, he's earning his pay today, isn't he?" Maddy asked.

"I'll let him go home early tonight," I said as I dialed his number.

"Eleanor, if you're going to keep waking me up,

I might as well come in and work," he said with a laugh when he answered.

"This will just take a second. I need to know if Samantha Stout and Kenny Stout are married to each other, or if they're just related in some other way."

"That I can do," he said. After a short pause, he said, "They were married. I guess technically they still are, since they have to wait another few months before the decree is final. The cause was filed as irreconcilable differences, whatever that means these days. Is there anything else I can do?"

"No, that's perfect. Go back to sleep."

"I would if I could, but I have a class at noon, so I might as well go ahead and get up now."

That was also when we opened, and I saw by my clock that I had four minutes until it was time to unlock the front door. "You'd better hurry up, then. You're going to miss class."

"Sorry, Mom. I'm leaving right now," he said with a hint of laughter in his voice.

I didn't even get the chance to answer before he hung up on me.

"What did he say?" Maddy asked.

"They were married, but they're separated now. I wonder if Grant had anything to do with that."

"Let me just say that it wouldn't surprise me if he had," she said. "What should we do next?"

I pointed to the clock. "Sorry, but our investigating time is over. We have to open the Slice now."

"Don't apologize. I'm kind of looking forward to serving a little pizza and soda. It might help take my mind off what a nightmare my life has become lately."

"Don't worry, Sis," I said as I hugged her. "We'll figure this out."

"I hope so," she said.

"In the meantime, let's sell some pizza. What do you say?"

"Open the doors, Eleanor. I'm ready for whatever comes our way today."

Only she wasn't.

To be fair, neither was I, but I had no idea what I was letting myself in for when I unlocked the front door of my pizzeria.

But it didn't take long for me to find out.

Chapter 7

"I figured I'd find you hiding in here," a woman who looked vaguely familiar to me said to Maddy as soon as we opened the door for business. She was pretty enough in an angular kind of way, and it was clear from the first moment she walked through the door that she thought she was better than anyone who dared look in her direction. The brunette brushed past me as though I were nothing but a doorman and headed straight for my sister. "Why did you have to kill him? You already got what you wanted. You somehow managed to brainwash my mother and my brother, but you never fooled me, not once."

"Hello, Rebecca. I'm sorry for your losses," Maddy told the woman, who was clearly none other than

Grant's sister. There was no doubt in my mind that she was also the one who'd nearly caught us snooping around at Sharon Whitmore's home earlier that day, but I wasn't about to bring that up.

"Save your phony condolences for someone who doesn't know you, Maddy," Rebecca snapped.

"Listen, maybe it would be a good idea for you to leave," I said as I started trying to shepherd her out of the restaurant. Even though no one was there yet, I still didn't want her attacking Maddy at the Slice.

"You can't make me go anywhere," she said angrily.

"That's where you're wrong," I said as I pointed to a sign behind the cash register. I'd had it installed after a particularly ugly visit a few months before, and it was plain and simple, declaring that I reserved the right to refuse service to anyone I chose to, whenever I pleased, without having any particular reason at all. I hadn't had to use it yet, but I had a hunch that it was about to come in handy. "In case you were wondering who that's referring to, at the moment it means you."

"Eleanor Swift, this doesn't concern you, so I'd appreciate it if you'd mind your own business."

"That's where you're wrong. When it comes to my sister, everything is my business."

Maddy spoke up. "Eleanor, I can handle her."

"Okay, if you're sure," I said. I took a few steps back, but there was no way that I was going to leave the dining room. It was hard to tell what might happen if I did that.

"I'm positive," Maddy said.

"Don't be so sure of yourself," Rebecca said. "I asked you a question, and I expect an answer. Why did you kill Grant? He was out of your life. There was no need to stab him with that skewer."

"I didn't stab him, and neither did Bob Lemon," Maddy said. She was trying to keep her cool, but I could see the red coming into her cheeks.

"If your supposed fiancé did it, it was still because of you. You might not have plunged that steel through his heart, but that doesn't mean that you weren't a part of it." She fumbled into her oversized purse and pulled out a piece of paper. "For the first time in your life, do the decent thing and sign this."

I glanced over Maddy's shoulder and saw that it was another quitclaim deed, just like the one Grant had forged the day before.

"What is it with you two?" Maddy demanded, losing the last bit of her restraint. "So what if Sharon left me some slides, a few teacups, and some other knickknacks? I know she was your mother, but she was my friend, too, and if she wanted me to have some worthless dishware and a few slides that you and Grant hated, I can't see why you feel the need to keep me from getting them."

"Don't try to act stupid, Maddy. It doesn't become you."

"I just wish I *was* acting," my sister said, the exasperation thick in her voice. "Rebecca, I honestly have no idea what you're talking about."

"My mother, either through coercion on your part or senility in her old age, left you a third of everything she owned. Now that Grant's dead, I guess it's half." Rebecca took a step back as she asked, "Do I have something to worry about now? Are you after *all* of it?"

"All of what?" Maddy shouted.

"We've all known for years that there's over a quarter of a million dollars in all of my mother's holdings," Rebecca said, "but don't think for one second that you're ever going to see one penny of any of it."

"That is so utterly ridiculous that I don't even know how to respond to it," Maddy said.

"Then sign this, and I'll get out of your life forever. Put your signature where your mouth is."

"I won't give you the satisfaction," Maddy said.

Rebecca rolled her eyes. "Why am I not surprised that you'd say that? That's a nice little righteous indignation you've got going there, Maddy. Too bad it's not going to do you any good. You're nothing but some kind of worthless scavenger."

"You're the only vulture I see in this room," Maddy said, finally letting her temper loose completely. "If she wanted me to have something, then I'm going to see that I get it."

"I won't take that, especially not from you!" Rebecca yelled as she reached for the nearest weapon in sight, which happened to be a full napkin holder. The weight of it was bad enough, but it also had several sharp edges, and I knew that if she hit my sister with it, it could do some real damage.

"What's going on here?" Kevin Hurley asked as he burst through the door. He looked at Rebecca and saw her makeshift weapon. "Put that down, and I mean right now."

Rebecca seemed to fold under the police chief's stinging words, and she put the napkin holder back on the tabletop where it belonged. "I wasn't going to do anything with it."

"Sure you weren't," Maddy said.

"Chief, I'd appreciate it if you'd do us a favor and escort Ms. Whitmore off the property," I said.

"Hang on a second," Rebecca said. "She can't just throw me out, no matter what that sign says."

"Ma'am, maybe it would be for the best if you came with me," Chief Hurley said as he gently put his arm in Rebecca's. "There are a few things we need to go over at the police station, and I know that you want to take care of them as soon as possible."

"What kind of things?" she asked.

"There's paperwork to be filled out, and you'll need to contact a funeral home to take charge of your brother," Kevin said, his words both soft and urging at the same time. I forgot sometimes just what a charmer our police chief could be when it suited him.

"Fine. I'll come with *you*," she said, and I thought for a second that we were going to get rid of her without any more commotion. But, of course, that wasn't about to happen. Rebecca hesitated at the door of the pizzeria and then turned back to face Maddy. "This isn't over, not by a long shot."

"I'm here every day we're open," Maddy replied, "so you always know where to find me."

"Go on," I said, urging her to get out before things turned nasty again.

Rebecca clearly didn't appreciate that, though. "I'm not about to forget the way you've treated me, too, Eleanor. You'd both better be careful."

"Come on," Chief Hurley said, this time putting a little more force into his voice.

"No need to push. I'm leaving," she said, and the two of them walked out together.

"We'd better be careful," Maddy said as she shook her head. "That threat sounded pretty serious. I'm not usually worried about people like Rebecca, but there was a crazy glint in her eyes."

"We'll be extra careful from now on," I answered, thinking about what Art had said.

"Can you believe that woman?" Maddy asked as she straightened the skewed napkin holder.

"Was she serious about the inheritance? Could Sharon have really left you an equal share of all that money?"

"I honestly don't know," Maddy said. "She always told me that I was the perfect daughter. It was something that used to steam Rebecca to no end. I didn't do anything to encourage it, but Rebecca always thought I was behind it. I could maybe understand it if Grant and I were still married, but you know as well as anybody how ugly our divorce was. What was she thinking, leaving me anything that substantial?"

"Maybe she just never got around to changing her will," I suggested.

Maddy smiled at me briefly. "Does that mean that you don't think she was that enamored with me, either? Why not? I'm adorable."

"Of course you are," I said, "but it could explain why she kept you in her will after all these years. Were you serious about what you said to Rebecca?"

"Which part?" she asked.

"That you are going to fight for what is rightfully yours. Don't get me wrong. I've got your back either way. I'm just curious, I guess."

"I guess that depends," Maddy said. "If Sharon wanted me to have such a healthy chunk of what she had, I'd be betraying her by refusing it, at least in my mind. On the other hand, if she simply forgot to change her will and take me out of it, how can I accept anything in good conscience?"

"I totally get what you're saying, but how can you possibly ever know?"

"I have no idea," she said as she shook her head. "But I'm not touching a dime of any of it until I can figure it out one way or the other."

* * *

"Are you open?" a man asked as he and his teenage daughter came into the Slice.

"Come on in," I said. "Welcome to the Slice."

"Thanks," he answered, though he looked a little shaky as he did so.

Maddy seated them, but before I could make it into the kitchen, he rushed over to me. "I understand that you're the owner."

"I am," I said.

"Listen," he said, his voice softened so that his daughter couldn't hear, "I was wondering if you had anything a little stronger than soda that you could slip into my Coke."

I'd heard the request before, though not often. "I'm sorry, sir, but we don't serve mixed drinks here."

He frowned a little and then asked, "Is there any place around here that does?"

"Not at this time of day," I replied. There was a bar on the outskirts of town, but I knew from general knowledge that they didn't open until three. This guy had to be some kind of alcoholic. "Excuse me for saying so, but should you really be drinking with your daughter in the car?"

"Why do you think I need one?" he asked. "I've never had a drink in my life, but I've been teaching her to drive for the past two days, and suddenly I've never wanted anything more in my life." He glanced back at his daughter, gave her a little wave, and then said to me, "Look at her, sitting there all innocent."

I glanced in his daughter's direction and saw a petite brunette who still had braces shining from her smile. "She's adorable," I said.

"You'd think so, but the truth is, she's trying to kill me." He said it with such complete sincerity that I had a hard time not believing him.

"Are you sure you're not just exaggerating?"

"I'm positive. At first she was going for a heart attack, tailgating other drivers, running red lights, and generally being a hazard on the road, but when that didn't work, she became a little more proactive. I swear, she claims she didn't see the bulldozer, but it was clear enough to me to read the T-shirt on the guy who was driving it. If I hadn't screamed in time, I'd be on the side of his blade instead of here with you."

"Maybe someone else could teach her?" I suggested.

"Would you?" he asked as I saw a flicker of hope come across his terrified face. "I'd pay you, and I mean well. How much is it worth to you?"

"I didn't mean me," I said hastily. "But surely there are instructors at her school."

He shook his head sadly. "None of them will ride with her. And before you suggest it, I tried private lessons, too. The word is out in this part of the state to watch out for her, and I can't blame them one bit."

"How about her mother, then?"

He looked visibly shaken by the suggestion. "Are you kidding? Where do you think she gets it?

If one of them doesn't get me, the other one will. Are you sure you don't have anything strong to drink?"

"Sorry I can't help you," I said.

"That's okay. I was foolish enough to believe that I might have a chance at all."

Josh came in as we were talking, and the man focused sharply on him. "Could he teach her, do you think?"

"I don't know," I said, "but maybe you should . . ."

He never waited to find out what I was going to suggest, but he probably wouldn't have liked it, anyway. I was going to say that it might do to wait a year or two, but it was clear by his daughter's intent expression that she wasn't about to take no for an answer.

"How would you like to make a hundred bucks?" the man asked as he approached Josh.

"Who do I have to kill?" Josh asked with a smile.

"Nobody. At least I hope not. Come over here. I'd like you to meet my daughter."

Josh took a step back. "Mister, I don't know what you have in mind, but I don't want to be any part of it. I'm not going to date your daughter for money."

"Date? Who said anything about dating? She's too young for that."

Maybe in her dad's eyes, but it was clear that the young lady was instantly smitten with Josh, if the way she was looking at him was any indication.

"What do I have to do, then?"

"Can you drive?"

"Like a pro," Josh said proudly.

"Then teach her."

Josh looked at me and asked, "Is he serious?"

"He is, but you might want to think about it before you say yes."

Josh turned back to the man. "You don't even know me. Why are you willing to entrust your daughter to me?"

"I recognized you the second you walked through the door. You're the police chief's son," the man said quickly. "I've heard good things about you."

I was willing to bet that he would have let Rasputin teach his daughter if it meant that he didn't have to. "You can always say no," I told Josh.

"I don't think so." He stuck a hand toward the man and said, "Mister, you've got yourself a deal."

"Excellent. Here are the keys. Don't worry about me. I'll get a ride back home on my own."

Josh was clearly puzzled by this reaction. "I'd like to help you out, Sir, but I've got to work my shift. Sorry."

The man wasn't about to accept that, though. He looked at me and said, "I'll pay you for an hour of his time. Please don't say no. If you want me to, I'll wait tables and wash dishes while they're gone. I'm begging you. I'm desperate."

I just couldn't bring myself to say no. I nodded,

and Josh walked over to the young woman. "How would you like a driving lesson?"

"With you? Absolutely," she said. "Thanks, Daddy," she said quickly as she and Josh left.

Maddy had been listening to the whole exchange. "Well done, Eleanor. You just blew a sale for us."

"I'll cover it gladly," the man said as he pulled out his wallet. He gave me two twenties and then put a hundred on top of them. "That will cover the lesson, the bill, and his wages. Are we square?"

"We are," I said as I collected the money. "Can one of us at least give you a ride home?"

"Are you kidding? I'm walking. Ha ha ha ha. Walking. How wonderful."

Once he was gone, I started having second thoughts about the arrangement. "Do you think Josh is going to be okay?"

"From the way that girl was looking at him, I think he'll be fine. What an odd dad he was."

"Remember Dad teaching us how to drive?" I reminded my sister.

"He thought we were trying to give him a heart attack," Maddy said.

"Then you've heard his song before, too."

I kept watching the door of the pizzeria as the hour nearly ended, and once, when I heard an ambulance in the distance, I nearly jumped out of my skin. Ten minutes after the hour lapsed, I was about to call Kevin Hurley and admit what I'd done, but just then Josh walked into the pizzeria with a grin on his face. "That was the easiest hundred I've ever made. He said you were holding it for me."

I slipped him the hundred and then added a twenty, as well.

He looked at the money and asked, "Hey, what's the bonus for?"

"Hazard pay," I said with a smile. "How bad was she?"

"I don't know what he was talking about. She's really very good. I even let her drive to her house, and I caught a ride back here with her dad. He was falling all over himself, he was so happy."

"Do you have any more lessons planned?" Maddy asked.

"First thing Saturday morning, we're going out for three hours. Wow, I never dreamed that making money could be this easy."

"You're not gouging him, are you?" I asked.

"I tried to tell him he was paying me too much, but the man wouldn't listen. He's really an odd bird." Josh spotted a table that needed to be cleaned. "Well, I'd better get to work. Thanks for the job, Eleanor."

"You're welcome, I think," I said.

I didn't know why I was always surprised when

unusual things happened at my pizza place, but I was.

At least this one had ended well for Josh, the man, and his daughter.

It wasn't always that things worked out so nicely for everyone.

Chapter 8

We were nearing the end of our afternoon lunch shift and approaching our own break for a meal, and I was up front, discussing with Maddy what we were going to do with our time off, when I looked up to see a familiar couple walk into the Slice, though it was the first time they'd ever been in my pizza place to my knowledge. They were in their civilian clothes now, and the woman's makeup was toned down quite a bit, but I had no trouble recognizing the Stouts, two of the performers we'd seen onstage the night before at the Founders Day Festival.

The woman approached me first. "Are you Eleanor Swift?"

"I am," I said. "I've got to say, you made yourself a fan last night. You all were really good onstage."

Samantha grinned a little at the compliment. "Thanks. We're still working on it, but I think we're finally getting there. Listen, Kenny and I were wondering if you had time to have a little chat."

Maddy wanted to stay, but a man at one of her tables was making writing signs in the air and looking frantic about it. "Would you mind taking care of that?" I asked her.

My sister wasn't all that pleased about it, but she still managed to smile. "Of course."

After she was gone, I said, "We've still got ten minutes before we close up shop for the afternoon, so if you're willing to hang around, we can talk as soon as we lock up."

"We'll make it easy on you. How about if we order a medium pie with the works and a couple of beers, and we can talk while we eat?"

"Sorry, but we don't sell beer," I said. "We have underage employees working here."

"Fine," she said, clearly trying to keep her smile. "Bring us some sodas, then. I've heard wonderful things about your food, and I'm dying to try some of your pizza."

"Are you kidding me? What's pizza without beer? This is a joke," Kenny said.

The woman turned to her ex-husband and said, "They don't have to talk to us at all. We're asking them for a favor, remember? Try to be civilized for once in your life and stop insulting them, would you?"

"Sam, give me a break."

Her expression iced over. "I told you that my name is now Samantha to you, and I expect you to use it. You're not entitled to give me pet names anymore."

She held his stare, and I wondered which one would back down. To no great surprise, Kenny dropped his gaze first.

"Okay, I got it. I'm sorry," he said.

"Good," she said. "Now, why don't you find us a table so I can talk to Eleanor alone for a second?"

He didn't like it, that much was clear, but he did as he was told.

Once he was out of hearing range, Samantha told me, "I could never train him like that when we were married. Maybe if I had, it would have lasted longer than it did. Are you married, Eleanor?"

"I was," I answered simply.

"Got rid of him too, did you? That's the only smart thing to do when one won't obey you."

I wasn't about to let her talk about Joe like that. "Actually, he died. I would give anything I possess to have him back." It was the complete truth, too. Sure, David was becoming more and more important to me every day, but no matter how close we got, it would be nearly impossible for me to love him as much as I had cared for Joe. That might not be fair to David, but I'd pretty much told him the same thing when we first got together, and he'd been willing to accept it. I knew that David hoped that I'd change my mind someday, and I was certainly willing to try, but it was hard to give up the past and focus on the future instead.

"I'm so sorry," Samantha said, the glibness now gone. "I get so full of myself sometimes that I forget that other people have had their share of woes, too. Can you forgive me?"

Wow, when this woman turned on the charm, it was palpable. "You're forgiven. Now, if you'll excuse me, I'll go make that pizza."

"We truly appreciate it," Samantha said and then joined her ex-husband.

I went back into the kitchen to make her pizza, and Maddy followed me in. "What was that all about? I can't believe that chucklehead couldn't just leave a ten on the table and be done with it."

"You didn't miss much. The Stouts want to chat, so we'll chat," I said as I knuckled the dough into the pan for their pizza.

"I heard that much. I'm just wondering what happened after they ordered."

"Nothing much," I said as I applied the sauce. "Why? Did they say something to you?"

"That's just it. She's sitting there in silence, and he looks like he's afraid to take a breath without permission. On second thought, that's how I'd like all my exes to be." Maddy realized what she was saying, and she quickly added, "I didn't mean it that way. I wasn't Grant's fan, but I'm still sorry that he's dead. You know that, don't you, Eleanor?"

"Of course I do," I said as I came from behind the counter and hugged her. "You don't have anything to explain to me. No matter what, I've always got your back, Maddy."

"I know that. As a matter of fact, I count on it," she replied as she hugged me back briefly and then let go. "What do you suppose they want to talk about?"

"Is there any doubt in your mind? It has to be about what happened to Grant last night."

"But why should they want to talk to us?" Maddy asked as I loaded on the toppings and then sent the pizza through the conveyor oven.

"I'm guessing they're in hot water with the police. Who knows? Maybe they saw us talking with Kevin Hurley and think we can help them, or maybe they've even heard about our crime-busting ways. I, for one, am glad that they showed up, whatever their reasoning is. It saves us the trouble of tracking them down ourselves."

"How hard should we push them?" Maddy asked as she picked up a sub that was waiting to be delivered.

"Let's take it easy at first. If things start to stall, we can always up the ante a little. Agreed?"

"As always, I defer to your judgment," Maddy said with no expression at all.

She held that look for barely one second before

she burst out laughing, and I was not far behind her.

Josh came through the kitchen door just then and asked, "What's going on?"

"More complications," I said.

"I was hoping to get something to eat before you break for lunch," he admitted. "That sub looks pretty good."

"Sorry. It's for a customer," I said, "but if you deliver it, I'll make one for you, too. How does that sound?"

"Wonderful. By the way, what were you two laughing about when I came in? If you know something I don't, I'd love to share in the joke myself."

"We were just being silly," Maddy said. "Don't mind us."

"Hey, as long as I'm not the target, I'm a happy camper." He reached for the sub. "Let me take that. You two can hang out some more."

"Don't worry. I've got it," Maddy said as she evaded his grasp. Maddy paused at the door and winked at me. "Thanks, Sis."

"You're most welcome."

Josh looked at me as he said, "You know, you two are the main reason I wish I had a sibling myself."

"You and Greg are close, aren't you?" I asked as I started cleaning up.

"Sure we are, but there's nothing like blood, is there?"

"No, sir, there's not. How many tables are full out there?" I knew he'd notice. Once you were used to monitoring a dining room, it was a tough habit to break.

"There are still three sets of customers, but I'm guessing that everyone left will be finished in less than five minutes, except for the pizza you just made."

It was time to make an executive decision. "Do me a favor, would you? Flip the sign and lock the door. With any luck at all, Maddy and I will be getting out early for lunch."

"I'll take care of it," Josh said as he hurried back out into the dining room.

I had a feeling that we were going to need all of the time that we could muster for this particular lunch hour. Not only did we need to speak with Samantha and Kenny Stout, but I also wanted to have a few words with Bernie Maine, if we could find him, that is. I had a hunch the man might be a bit elusive after what had happened to one of his business partners the night before, but if he was still in our part of North Carolina, Maddy and I would find him.

I plated and cut the pizza for Samantha and Kenny and grabbed some plates. I'd sent Josh on his way, with his sub and a soda, so the four of us had the place to ourselves.

Maddy was out front wiping down the tables and cleaning up in general, and she cut me off before I got too close to the exes.

"Have you been talking to them yet?" I asked her quietly.

"No. I decided to wait for you."

"That's a remarkable show of restraint on your part," I told her.

"Well, one of the reasons I waited was because they wouldn't answer any questions until the four of us were all together," she replied with a grin.

"So, not so much on the restraint part."

"Not so much," she agreed. "That pizza looks great. Did they order an extra-large? I thought they asked for a medium."

"No, but I went ahead and made one big enough for all of us. It might be easier to get them to open up if we all share a meal together."

"Did you ask them about it first?" Maddy asked me, probably a little louder than she'd intended.

"Ask us what?" Samantha asked. "Is that for us? If it is, it's way too big."

I walked to the table and put the pizza down in the middle. "This is the only lunch break we get, so we were kind of hoping that we could all eat together. It's on the house if you're willing to share it with us."

"Sold," Kenny said.

"Is that okay with you, too, Samantha?"

"Of course it is," she said.

Maddy grabbed us a couple of drinks and refilled theirs, and we sat down to have a bite to eat and to talk a little about murder.

"This is delicious even without the beer," Kenny said after he took his first bite.

"Because it's free, or you really think it's good?" Samantha asked him.

"Can't it be a little bit of both?" he asked, and then he took another bite.

I tried some, too, and he was right. My garbage pizzas were tasty, and it didn't hurt that I was starving. Most days I was fine making food for everyone else, but today was one of the times where I was tempted to nibble on everything I made, a strict no-no for a pizza chef.

As we ate, I decided to dive in and start the conversation. "So, what did you want to see us about?"

"We understand you two are nosing around into Grant's murder," Kenny said.

"Can you possibly be a little more tactful than that?" Samantha asked.

"We prefer to think of ourselves as amateur sleuths," Maddy said, "but yes, we're investigating his murder. As a matter of fact, if you hadn't walked into the Slice this afternoon, we were going to come looking for you."

"Why would you want to see us?" Samantha asked, watching us both closely. "We knew Grant, but neither one of us had anything to do with his murder. We were all friends."

"You were more than that," I said.

Kenny looked at Samantha with disdain. "I told

you they knew you were sleeping with the guy. So much for beating around the bush."

It was all I could do not to show my surprise about a physical relationship between Samantha and Maddy's ex-husband. My sister didn't even flinch, and she had a lot more reason to react to the news than I did.

"Who told you about us?" Samantha asked, not bothering to try to deny it.

"It wasn't all that hard to figure out," I said quickly before Maddy could comment. "We saw the way you were looking at Grant last night during your performance, and if there was any doubt in our minds, Kenny's reaction onstage sealed it for us."

"Let's get one thing straight," Samantha said. "Grant and I did have a fling, but our marriage was already over by the time it started. Isn't that right, Kenny?"

"So you say," her ex answered. It was clear that Kenny wasn't all that convinced, and neither was I.

"I won't keep defending my behavior, to you or anyone else," Samantha said. "It was a short, stupid thing between us, and when it ended, Grant and I both walked away without any hurt feelings or regrets."

"I'm willing to bet you were pretty upset about losing your investment, though," Maddy said to Samantha.

"You know about that, too?" she asked, clearly

surprised by our knowledge. "You two really are as good as we heard you were."

"How much did you lose?" I asked her.

"It wasn't all that bad. In the end, it totaled less than ten thousand dollars," she admitted.

I whistled. That had to be a good chunk of her savings if her prime source of income was playing at street fairs. "How much less?"

"Not much," Kenny said. "It was all from the divorce settlement Samantha got from me, so in a way, he ripped both of us off when he talked her into making that deal."

"But everyone lost money with Orion, didn't they?" Maddy said.

"Your sources aren't as good as you might think. Sure, we all lost out on paper, but I just found out that Grant discovered a way to pull most of the money out of the investment before Bernie found out and everything collapsed. He had no choice but to shut it all down. Grant had cash, and I wanted my share back. It's the reason we wanted to talk to him last night after our show," Samantha said.

"And did you?" I asked as I took another bite of pizza. The conversation was so intense that it was taking something out of the joy I normally found when eating one of my pizzas, but it couldn't be helped. These questions had to be asked.

"Sure, we finally managed to corner him, for all the good it did us. Grant claimed that *Bernie* was the double-crosser, not him, and what's more, he said that he had proof of it."

"What kind of proof?" Maddy asked.

"He wouldn't say, but he was pretty smug about the whole thing."

"Did you believe him?" I asked.

Kenny spoke up. "She wanted to, but not me. I didn't care who took that money. I just wanted it back."

"For me, you mean," Samantha said.

"For us. I was going to make you split it with me right down the middle if I managed to recover any of it."

"You have *got* to be kidding me," Samantha said, clearly surprised by this news. "What makes you think I would have ever agreed to that?"

"If you wouldn't have, I was going to keep it all," he said smugly.

"Over my dead body," she replied.

"Don't tempt me," he answered.

That was about all of the bickering I could take at the moment. "How about if we get this all back on track? From what you've just told us, you both had your own reasons to want to see Grant dead. Samantha, who decided to end the relationship between you and Grant?"

"I did," she said as Kenny answered at the exact same time, "He did."

"Which one of you is telling the truth?" Maddy asked.

"I was in the relationship, not *him*," she said as

she gestured toward Kenny. "As soon as I discovered that my investment was gone, I walked away."

"So, do you believe that Grant was the one with the money?" I asked.

"It didn't matter," Samantha said with a frown. "He's the one who talked me into investing in Orion in the first place, and when it all fell apart, he wouldn't make any kind of restitution. I dumped him the instant he refused to give me any of my money back."

"If that's true, then it must have happened pretty recently," Maddy said.

"I never claimed that it didn't," Samantha snapped at her. "I dumped him yesterday morning, and last night I was still trying to get my money back when we spoke with him at the concert."

"I'm amazed he let the two of you corner him like that," I said.

"Are you kidding? It was all Grant's idea. It's the only place he'd talk to us. There were a lot of people at that fair last night. I guess that made him feel that it was safe enough."

"Boy, was he ever wrong," Kenny said.

"We didn't kill him, though," Samantha said. "Someone else did."

"I know that, and you know that," Kenny answered, "but who's going to convince the police that we're innocent?"

"That's why we're here talking to Eleanor and Maddy, remember?" she said.

"Hang on a second," Maddy said, holding her

hands up for silence. "Are you telling us that you came by the Slice to ask us for help in proving that you're both innocent?"

"Why is that so hard to believe?" Kenny asked.

"Maybe because you two are at the top of our suspect list," Maddy blurted out.

"You're siding with the *police?*" Samantha asked.

"We're not taking sides," I said quickly. "We're after the truth, no matter who it might implicate."

"Even your precious fiancé?" Kenny asked Maddy.

"Bob didn't kill Grant," Maddy said flatly.

"How could you possibly know that? Are *you* his alibi?" Kenny asked.

"No," Maddy admitted, "but he doesn't need one, as far as I'm concerned. How about the two of you? If you want us to help you, we have to know where you were when Grant was murdered."

Either my sister was being brilliant or she'd completely lost her mind. Was she serious about even considering helping this pair? I decided to keep my mouth shut while she worked. Either way, I'd back her up one thousand percent, but I didn't know enough about what she was doing to make a play one way or the other.

"We're waiting," Maddy said. "Where were you?"

It was clear that Kenny didn't like the neat way she'd turned the tables on them. "Samantha, we don't have to answer that."

"We're asking them for help, don't you remember? She's right, Kenny. The only way we can expect them to lend us a hand is to tell them both what we were doing when Grant was murdered."

"You can tell them if you want to, but count me out of this," he said as he stood, threw his napkin on the table, and stormed out of the Slice. At least he tried to. He was locked in, though, so it took him five seconds to fumble with the latch before he could get out.

"I'm sorry about this. We'll be back," Samantha said as she hurried out the door after him.

I took another bite of pizza as we waited. "So, are we really helping them now?"

Maddy shook her head. "There's not a chance of that happening, but if I can get solid alibis for them, we can at least mark them off our list."

"If neither of them did it, that just leaves Bernie Maine. If."

"If what?"

"If we've found all of our suspects yet," I said.

"Who else did you have in mind?" Maddy asked as she took another bite of pizza.

"I don't know, but then again, we just started digging. It's hard to say who else might turn up on our suspect list. Grant had a way of riling folks up, didn't he?"

"It's a skill that he'd apparently gotten better at over the years."

"What do you think?" I asked her. "Could he have swindled other investors, as well?"

"It wouldn't surprise me one bit," she said. "Eleanor, I should have listened to you all those years ago. You saw right through him, and you tried to warn me, but I wouldn't listen."

"Don't beat yourself up about it, Maddy. I got lucky finding Joe, and now you've got Bob in your life. We all win some, and we lose some."

"I seem to have picked more than my share of losers over the years, though," she said. "As bad as Grant was when we were married, I never would have believed that he could take such a turn for the worse. Sharon must have been heartbroken."

"I'm sure she knew that she did what she could," I said as I glanced toward the door. "I'm not positive they're coming back, are you?"

"Oh, there's no doubt in my mind. They're gone for good," Maddy said as she took another bite of her pizza and then dropped it onto her plate. "Forgive me for throwing away your hard work, but I've kind of lost my appetite for this right now."

"I couldn't agree with you more," I said as I gathered everything together and headed for the nearest trash can.

"You're not chucking that because of me, are you?"

"No way. Maybe later I'll make us a different kind of snack, but right now I think we should get out of here while we still have the chance."

"Are we going to go out looking for Kenny and Samantha?" she asked me as I rinsed the plates in back.

"I've got a feeling that we're going to have to

wait until they're ready to talk to us, but I'd love to see if we can find Bernie Maine."

"In thirty minutes?" Maddy asked me.

"No, you're right. We need at least an hour and a half to get to Cow Spots and back and still talk to him. Why don't you put up a sign that we're going to be late starting our dinner shift tonight?"

"What are you going to be doing?"

"I'm calling Josh to give him a heads-up about what we're planning to do," I said. "There's no reason to make him wait out front for us while we're somewhere out of town, digging into murder."

After we had wrapped up what we needed to do in the kitchen and had told Josh about our plans, Maddy and I left the Slice in search of the elusive Bernie Maine.

Chapter 9

"I've got a question for you," Maddy said as we started driving my car toward the town of Cow Spots.

"Is it about the case?" I asked.

"No, it's about this place where we're heading. Why on earth would anyone ever call their hometown Cow Spots in the first place? It's a crazy thing to name a place, and that's even taking into consideration that North Carolina's known for some of its weird town names."

I laughed. "What did you do? Fall asleep in fifth grade North Carolina geography class? Don't you remember? That's when they taught us all kinds of things about the origins of different city and county names in the state."

"Ms. Harpold didn't cover any of that," Maddy said. "The ink was still wet on her diploma when she took over my class, so it's hard to say what all I missed out on. She'd had her heart set on teaching high school girls' phys ed, and at the last second, they stuck her with us. You had Mrs. Ingersoll, didn't you?"

"Oh, yes," I said, remembering the oldest teacher I'd ever had. "She had to be a hundred and five by the time she finally retired, but the woman was as sharp as she could be up until the last day of class."

"Then enlighten me, Eleanor."

"Well, there's nothing all that special about it, as far as I can remember it. According to Mrs. Ingersoll, the surveyor got lost in the middle of laying out the town limits and ended up making a mess of it. It looked sort of like a Holstein's spots, without a straight line anywhere in it. I heard later that he wasn't lost at all. He was just falling-down drunk. The place was named Cowton at the time, but the surveyor looked at the mess he'd made and registered it as Cow Spots to explain the lousy job he'd done, and somehow it stuck. From what I've heard, a few folks tried to change it officially back to Cowton when it first happened, but they never made much headway, so Cow Spots it has been ever since."

"It's not really a *great* story, is it?" Maddy asked.

"Hey, it is what it is. Do you think we'll be able to track Bernie Maine down once we get to town?"

"It's hard to say. I don't know much about the

131

place. I wonder if Kevin Hurley has managed to speak with him yet."

"I'm not even sure he knows that Bernie should be on his suspect list yet," I admitted. "Sometimes I wish we both shared what we discovered with each other, instead of playing cat and mouse with the facts, you know?"

"Sis, you and I both know that it's never going to happen," Maddy said.

"Hey, we've compared notes a few times in the past," I protested.

"Okay, not never. How about rarely? The police chief ordinarily doesn't like us butting into his active investigations. You know what? If I were in his shoes, I wouldn't want us digging around, either. When I think about it, I'm amazed that he's been as understanding with us as he has in the past."

"Kevin knows deep down that we're just trying to help," I said.

Maddy laughed. "Maybe a little too much at times, right?"

"Hey, we are what we are. No excuses, no explanations."

We pulled alongside the Cow Spots town limit sign and were greeted by a twelve-foot fiberglass Holstein cow. It had become the official mascot of the place, and you could even buy hats and T-shirts with the cow's picture on them.

Initially, I decided not to stop in at the visitors' center to make any purchases, but at the last second, I pulled off in front of the trailer that acted as a welcome to outsiders visiting the place for the first time.

"This is an odd time to stop and get a magnet in the shape of a cow for your refrigerator," Maddy said. "Why are we pulling over here?"

"As far as I can figure, I believe that it's as good a place as any to start tracking down Bernie Maine. If anybody knows where we can find him, it might just be in there," I said as I put the car in park and shut off the engine. "Are you coming?" I asked her.

"Oh, I wouldn't miss seeing it for the world. I'm right behind you."

We walked into the small building and were instantly assaulted by all things cow related. As I suspected, there were T-shirts, sweatshirts, bandannas, hats of all kinds, and other merchandise emblazoned with black spots on white backgrounds. That was just the start of it, though. There were also magnets, key chains, shot glasses, and every other kind of knickknack imaginable, all with the same bovine theme.

"Excuse me, but do you happen to have anything with a cow on it?" Maddy asked the older woman sitting behind the counter, who was reading a magazine, one on dairy farming, of all things.

She grinned. "To tell you the truth, I'd be hard-pressed to come up with something that didn't bear the markings of our mascot," she said. "What can I do for you ladies?"

"We're looking for a man named Bernie Maine," I said.

Her smile suddenly disappeared as her gaze went back to the magazine. "Sorry. I can't help you."

"We're not here to give him a bouquet of flowers," Maddy said. "He might have had something to do with my ex-husband's recent murder, and we want to talk to him before he tucks his tail between his legs and runs."

"You were married to Grant Whitmore?" she asked, studying my sister with a critical glance as she put her magazine down.

"I'm not proud of the fact, but I was indeed. I finally have a good man in my life now, but he's under suspicion for Grant's murder, and if I can help him, I will."

She smiled and nodded when she heard my sister's answer. "Then you'd better hurry. I heard through the grapevine that he was packing up his office and getting ready to head out of town for good."

"Where can we find him?" I asked.

"Leave your car here. His place is four doors down that way. It's called BEM Enterprises."

"Thanks," I said.

"No time for pleasantries. Go!"

We did as she suggested, and as we neared the building in question, we found a man loading the back of his BMW with boxes.

When he turned to go back for more, I wasn't all that surprised to find that it was the same man we'd seen arguing with Grant in the shadows of the fair the night before.

Apparently, Bernie Maine had the opportunity, the means, and the motive to get rid of Maddy's ex-husband. And now he was trying to escape.

Maddy was starting after him when I put a hand on her arm.

"What are you doing, Eleanor? We can't just stand here and let him get away."

"How are we going to stop him? I have to call Kevin and see if he has any connections in town. The only way Bernie's not going to run is if we have the police stop him."

"Dial fast, then," she said.

I called Kevin Hurley, and after his gruff response, I said, "You can chew me out later for digging into something that's none of my business, but do you know that Bernie Maine, Grant's former business partner, is getting ready to leave town?"

"Where is he?" Kevin said. "What's he doing in Timber Ridge?"

"He's not. He's packing up his office in Cow Spots, and it looks like it's for good. Do you know anybody here that could slow him down until you can get here yourself to question him? If we have to, Maddy and I will stand in front of his car so he can't pull out, if you think that would help."

"Don't do anything stupid," Kevin said. "I'm on it." And then he hung up.

"What did he say?" Maddy asked after I put my phone back in my pocket.

"He told us not to do anything stupid," I answered, relaying the message.

"Well, he's going to have to be a lot more specific than that," she said just as the business's door opened again. Bernie Maine was coming out with a briefcase under his arm and an overnight bag in his free hand. He locked his office and was heading for his car when Maddy said, "I'm sorry, Eleanor, but we can't wait another minute."

Before I could stop her, she rushed toward Maine, somehow managing to get between him and his car.

The man was clearly startled by her behavior, and with good reason, in my opinion. My sister could be a real force to reckon with when she put her mind to it. "Who are you, and what do you want?" he asked. It was clear from his voice that she'd really shaken him up with her abrupt and sudden appearance. The man was jumpy. There was no doubt about that.

"I want to talk to you about Grant Whitmore," she said as I joined her. If it was possible, he was even less pleased to see that now there were two of us blocking his way.

"I don't have anything to say to you, or anyone else, about my former partner," Maine said harshly.

"Yeah, well, I'm his former wife, so that trumps your position to keep quiet," Maddy said. "Talk, buster."

He looked taken aback by that bit of information, so I decided to turn up the heat even more. "We saw you arguing with him last night in Timber Ridge, at the fair," I added, "so we know that you had contact with him, and recently."

"That's impossible. You're clearly mistaken. I wasn't anywhere near there."

"There's no use lying. We both saw you there," I said.

"You might have thought you did, but you are wrong. I'm going now, so I'd advise you both to stay out of my way." Bernie Maine looked as though he would push us both to get to his car, so I tugged on Maddy's arm and pulled her out of the way.

"We can't just let him go," she protested.

"We don't have any choice." Despite what I'd told Chief Hurley, I wasn't about to do anything as drastic as trying to stop him by force. Where were our reinforcements? Was Bernie Maine going to just drive away? I had a hunch that he'd be impossible to find once he left town.

The BMW started and was beginning to pull away when a police car suddenly appeared, neatly cutting off the luxury car's escape.

Maine got out at the same time that the officer did, and from the redness of his face, he was about to start screaming.

The cop cut him off, though. "Mr. Maine, the chief asked me to hold you here until he gets a chance to come by, and I'd consider it a personal favor if you did it voluntarily."

"And if I don't?"

"Well, if you really want to play it that way, then I'll just have to find a way to persuade you," the deputy said, a hint of steel in his voice now. It was clear there was no love lost between the two men, and I wondered how far the cop was willing to push it.

We didn't have to find out.

Ten seconds later another police car came around the corner, and this one had markings that indicated this was the chief of police of Cow Spots himself.

It appeared that the law had come to the rescue, after all.

I just hoped that all this effort was worth the tongue-lashing I knew that I was going to get from our chief of police.

"I didn't do anything!" I heard Bernie Maine say in protest the moment the chief of police got out of his cruiser. He was a handsome and fit man, with dark hair cropped short and his eyes covered by sunglasses.

"Now, hold on, Mr. Maine. Nobody's accusing you of anything, at least not just yet. I'd like to ask you a few questions, and as a matter of fact, so would a colleague of mine from Timber Ridge. Now, it's probably only fair to tell you that I can't make you hang around, but I guarantee you one thing. If you don't cooperate, I'll be an unhappy man, and believe me, you don't want that. Now, are you going to pull your car back all the way into that driveway and wait with us, or do we have to do this in a more official manner? The choice is yours, but if you decide to make things difficult, I'll make sure that Officer Petty handles you personally."

We all glanced at the deputy, whose grin was unmistakable. "That's the choice I'm hoping you make." It was clear that Maine got the not-so-subtle warning.

Maine threw his hands up into the air. "Have it your way. I'll be in my car, but I won't wait long, and in the meantime, I'm calling my attorney."

"Call anybody you'd like to," the chief said. "Just don't try to leave."

As Maine did as he was told, the chief turned to Petty and said, "Watch him."

"Yes, sir," the deputy said as he started walking toward the BMW.

"Nicely," the chief called out loudly.

"Yes, sir," his officer acknowledged, though this time there was quite a bit less enthusiasm in his voice as he said it.

The chief of police shrugged as he explained, "Officer Petty's mother lost money as a minor investor in one of Maine's companies. I don't think the man wants to take any chances with my deputy, not if he knows what's good for him." The chief smiled at us both, removing his sunglasses as he did. His dark brown eyes had the same flecks of gold in them that my late husband had, and that made me feel warmly toward the lawman, no matter how crazy that might sound. "Ladies, I'm Chief Hudson, but you may call me Stephen."

"Hi, Chief," I said, despite his offer to be a little less formal. "Thanks for coming to the rescue. I suppose you want to know what this is all about."

"Actually, Chief Hurley already filled me in," he said as he glanced at his watch. "He should be here in ten minutes." The grin dampened slightly as he added, "I'm afraid he's not very pleased with the two of you."

"I'm not at all surprised," I said. "I've got a feeling we probably deserve it."

"Well, as long as you aren't misbehaving in my jurisdiction, I don't have a problem with either one of you." Then he looked over at the BMW and added, "I guess that's exactly what you're doing, though, isn't it?"

I was about to explain when he held up a hand, demanding immediate silence, which I gave him. The chief continued, "I understand that this might just be justified, though. I'm sorry for your loss."

I was afraid my sister would take that opportunity to make a smart reply, but thankfully, all she said was, "Thank you."

Chief Hudson pointed to the BMW. "Your chief didn't exactly have to twist my arm, anyway. I've had my eye on this joker for the last year, but I can never seem to nail him on anything. If he leaves town and never comes back, I could live with that, but if he's killed someone, then we need to get him, and get him good." As he said the last bit, there was a deeper hint of iron in his voice, and I knew that I didn't want to cross him, ever. He might live and enforce the laws in a town that had a funny name, but there was nothing clownish about this man.

A minute later a familiar squad car hurried up toward us, and I didn't need to see who was driving to know that it was our own Timber Ridge chief of police.

He got out of the car and walked straight toward us, but Maddy and I got none of his attention. Instead, he headed for his counterpart and stuck out his hand. "Chief, it's good to see you again. Thanks for the backup."

"Always glad to lend a hand, Chief," Chief Hudson answered. "I'd be happy for you to talk to Maine here, or you can use my office in town. It's just a few blocks away, and it might make a bigger impression on the man if you do that, though I doubt it."

"No, I think this will be fine," Chief Hurley said. He turned and walked toward the black BMW without a word, a gesture, or even a glance in our direction.

"Good luck, ladies," Chief Hudson said to us as he offered us an imaginary tip of the hat and then walked after our chief of police.

"Too many chiefs, not enough Indians," Maddy said as soon as he was out of hearing range. "I've been dying to say that since Kevin Hurley first drove up."

"I'm glad you managed to restrain yourself as long as you did," I said, glancing over at the car. Kevin Hurley was now in the car's passenger seat, and Chief Hudson was sitting in the back, behind Bernie Maine. I would have felt sorry for the man except for the fact that he might have killed Maddy's ex-husband. As it was, he was a crook who most likely deserved everything he got, if even half the stories we had heard about him were true.

After three minutes the doors to the car opened, and the two chiefs got out. Chief Hudson said something to his deputy, who reluctantly moved his car out of the way so Bernie Maine could drive off.

"You're just letting him go after all the trouble we went to, to find him?" Maddy asked loudly.

Chief Hurley held a warning finger up to her, and she backed off immediately. Maddy knew as well as I did that there were times when we could push him and times when we could not. This was clearly one of those latter times.

Bernie Maine drove away, and so did Chief Hudson and his deputy.

At least Chief Hurley waited until they were gone before he finally approached us.

"Of all the harebrained, risky, senseless, and stupid things you two have ever done, this is the topper of them all. What were you thinking?"

"We're trying to catch a killer. What are *you* thinking?" Maddy asked, the outrage full in her voice.

"Maddy, take a deep breath and think about it. What if your suspicions are right and that man is a killer? Does it make any sense at all to confront him alone? What would keep him from coming after the two of you if he really is the killer?"

I did what he suggested and considered it for a moment, and then I realized that perhaps we had been a little rash. "We're sorry," I said as contritely as I could manage.

"We are?" Maddy asked, her tone of voice showing that she was still ready for a fight.

I shook my head slightly, and she folded in a little on herself.

"What she said," Maddy said as she pointed to me. "We're sorry."

"Good. I accept your apologies," Chief Hurley said with a nod. "And it's never going to happen again, right?" When we didn't answer, he asked the question again. "Right?"

"That we won't promise, and you know it," I said. "We don't want to lie to you. But our intentions were good here."

"Don't get me started on where good intentions lead," he answered.

"Okay, we get it. Consider us scolded," I said. "Did Bernie Maine tell you anything important?"

I wasn't sure what reaction I was expecting from my question, but the laughter I got in reply wasn't even on the list. "You two take the cake. You know that, don't you?"

"Hey, he'd have been long gone if it wasn't for us. Come to think of it, he *is* long gone, so I guess we didn't do any good at all," Maddy said.

"I wouldn't go that far," Chief Hurley said. "We have a meeting scheduled for tomorrow morning in my office."

"What makes you think he'll show up?" I asked.

"He's not stupid," the chief said. "He clearly hadn't thought it through, getting ready to just take off like that. Maine panicked, and I reminded him that the best thing he could do was stick around and see what happens."

"The guy's a con man," Maddy said loudly. "What makes you think that you can believe a single word he says?"

"He'll show up, because his attorney had already told him the same thing that we did. There's no doubt in my mind we can trust him, at least that far."

I didn't know if I was as accepting of that as the chief was, but I knew that if I didn't get Maddy out of there, she was going to get us both into even more trouble. Though she'd echoed my apology, even I had doubted the sincerity of it.

As my sister started to reply, I nudged her gently and the chief said, "I thought you two had a pizza place to run. Josh has a shift this evening, right?"

"He does, and you're right. We shouldn't keep

him waiting. We'll see you back in town. Thanks for coming."

Maddy was clearly not ready to leave, but I put my arm in hers and started walking her back down the street, toward the welcome center.

"Why did you let him off so easily?" Maddy asked me once we were far enough down the block.

"Do you honestly believe that fighting with our chief of police was going to get us anywhere? We have to choose our battles, Maddy. This one was already lost, so there was no need pushing it any harder."

"But now we'll never hear Maine's alibi," my sister protested.

"I have a feeling we'll get it sooner than you think," I said.

"Why would the chief loosen up about that?"

"He knows we gave him a good tip," I said as we got into the car and started back to Timber Ridge. "There's a good chance that he'll reciprocate, but if we'd badgered him anymore, he wouldn't have told us a thing."

"How do you know him so well?" Maddy asked.

"Hey, we dated a long, long time ago, remember?"

"And you don't think he's changed any since high school?"

"Oh, he's changed in more ways than I could count, but I still believe that the Kevin Hurley I used to know is still buried somewhere under that uniform."

"You're not getting romantic feelings about him again, are you?" Maddy asked with a suspicious expression on her face.

I laughed so hard that I nearly drove off the road. "No way, no thanks. I've got a man in my life these days, remember?"

"I just wanted to make sure that you weren't going soft on me," Maddy said.

"You don't have a thing to worry about there."

"That's what I like to hear. What are we going to do next?"

I glanced at the clock on the dashboard and saw that it was time to go back to our pizzeria. "We're doing exactly what the chief of police suggested. We're heading back to the Slice and opening up for our evening crowd."

"If I'm going to be honest about it, sometimes I resent that place getting in the way of our investigations," Maddy said.

"Just remember, without A Slice of Delight, we'd have no way of supporting ourselves. It's vital that we keep the business going as strong as we can manage."

"You've got a point," Maddy said. "But we still have more leads to follow. We haven't even finished going through the things we found in Grant's room."

"I know that, and don't forget, we still need to

see exactly what was going on in her life when Sharon left you a third of everything she owned."

"I don't even want to think about that," Maddy said.

"You might not want to at this moment, but sooner rather than later, you're going to have to do just that."

Chapter 10

"We've got company," Maddy said when she came back into the kitchen a few hours after we'd returned from Cow Spots. We were in a bit of a lull at the moment, after a pretty good run of customers, and I'd been using the time to give my workstation a good scrub. Maddy liked to save her cleaning for the end of her shift when she worked the kitchen area, but I was a firm believer in keeping the place as clean as I could at all times.

"It's not Bernie Maine, is it?" I asked as I put down my rag, washed my hands, and slid a fresh calzone onto a plate for her to deliver. Between our customers and my cleaning, I hadn't had much of a chance to even think about Grant Whitmore's murder.

"Not even close," she said with a grin. She turned around and said, "Gentlemen, you can come on back now."

I was surprised when Bob and David walked in together. After glancing at the clock, I asked, "What are you two doing here this time of day? Shouldn't you both be working?"

Bob looked at David and asked, "Is she always this welcoming?"

"Well, to be fair, I don't usually just show up unannounced, so I couldn't say for sure," he replied and then winked at me. "If you want any more information than that, you're going to have to ask the lady yourself."

"Coward," Bob said with a slight smile.

"Nobody's answered my questions yet," I said.

"In all seriousness," Bob said, "we decided to cut out early to see if we could help you and Maddy with your investigation. After all, we both have a stake in this, too, me more than anyone else."

I thought about it and then looked at Maddy. "I'm not sure what I think about it, so I'm going to leave it up to you. It's your call, Sis."

"Why are you shoving the decision on me?"

"Grant was your ex," I said. "I'll go along with whatever you decide."

"Are you telling me that you don't even have an opinion about it?"

"I suppose that I do, when I think about it. Are you asking for it, Maddy?"

"I am."

"Then I say let them help, even if it's just a little bit," I replied.

"Wow, thanks for the warm words of encouragement and support," David said with a grin.

"Don't get me wrong. I know that you're both good at what you do. David, if you weren't, they wouldn't have put you in charge." Then I turned to Bob. "As for you, if I ever get in a legal jam, you will be the first person I call. But neither one of you has ever done this kind of investigating before."

"Eleanor, don't sell me short," Bob said. "A great deal of what I do is reading people and trying to get information from them that they might not necessarily want to share with me."

"Maybe so, but because of your status as an attorney, I'm willing to bet that folks aren't going to speak to you as freely as they do with Maddy and me. Sure, you can handle them on the stand, but my sister and I can get things out of them that they don't even realize they're divulging."

"I don't deny that about Bob, since he's got a legal standing around here," David said, "but nobody's going to suspect that I'm up to anything."

I hated to come out and say it, but he hadn't left me any choice. "David, you just moved here four years ago. Nobody's going to trust you enough yet to tell you anything."

"Wow, this place is as tight-knit as a small town in New England," David replied.

"I'm not saying that it's fair, but it's how things are," I said.

"Surely there are more ways that we can help than just by interviewing suspects," Bob said.

I thought about it and realized that Bob had a point. It was crazy not to get their input on what we'd found. They might have insights that my sister and I could have missed. "Maddy, do you mind if I share what we found with them?"

"No, go ahead. I'll be right back. I've got to deliver this calzone, and I don't want to leave Josh out there by himself. Is there any chance you could get Greg to come in so the four of us can do some sleuthing?"

"Sorry, but he's got a major exam he's studying for, and I hate to pull him away from his schoolwork. The test is tomorrow, so he's coming in tomorrow night for the dinner shift, but I can't get him here any sooner."

"That's fine. We'll just figure something else out as we go through the papers we've got," she said as she left the kitchen to deliver the food.

"What are these papers you're talking about?" Bob asked.

"Before I can show you anything, there's something you should know. We were doing a little snooping, and no one exactly gave us permission to look where we were hunting, so I don't want to hear one word of scolding or disapproval from either one of you. Is that agreed?"

Bob frowned as he shook his head. "Perhaps I didn't think this through thoroughly enough. It might be better if you didn't say another word. As an officer of the court, I'm duty bound not to participate in any illegal activity."

"I was afraid that might be the case," I said.

"So, are you saying that you *did* come by this information illegally?" Bob asked.

"I refuse to answer that on the grounds that I might incriminate myself and my sister," I said.

"You're not under oath, Eleanor."

"It doesn't matter. I'm still not answering." I took a step toward him and said, "Bob, Maddy and I both know the kind of pressure you're under right now. We've both been suspected of murder in the past, and we know that it's not fun. You're just going to have to trust that either we or Chief Hurley is going to catch this killer."

"I believe in you all, but it's so hard to just not do anything," he said.

"I'm sure that it is. Tell you what. If we come up with anything you *can* do to help, we'll ask you. I promise."

"I suppose it's going to have to be good enough," Bob said, clearly deflated.

"How about me?" David asked. "I never took any pledges or made any promises."

"You can help, if you insist, but to be honest with you, I'd like it better if you weren't involved, either."

David looked a little hurt by my statement, but there was nothing I could do about it.

After a moment's pause, he asked, "Might I ask why?"

"David, you were by yourself last night, just the same as Bob was. You could have had time to kill Grant and get over to my house without being seen, too."

He looked shocked by my statement. "But why would I do that? Eleanor, surely you don't think I'm capable of something like that."

"I didn't say that I thought that you did it," I hurried to reply. "I'm just saying that if folks find out that you're helping us, they might begin to wonder if you're just trying to cover your own tracks in this investigation."

"The same thing could be said of you and Maddy," David said calmly.

"David, honestly, that's not fair," Bob said.

"Actually, it's spot on," I admitted, "but the people around Timber Ridge are getting so used to Maddy and me digging into murder that I honestly believe it would make them more suspicious of us if we didn't look into what happened to Grant."

David frowned at me for a moment, eased up on it a bit, and then turned to Bob. "Come on, my friend. Let's get out of here and get a bite to eat somewhere else. It appears that our use to these ladies is strictly as ornamental arm candy."

"I don't know how I feel about being referred to that way," Bob said a little reluctantly.

"Relish it," David said with a grin. "That's what I'm planning to do."

"It's not like that. Honestly, it isn't," I protested, but David just winked at me as he led Bob out of the kitchen.

Maddy came back a few minutes later. "What happened, Eleanor? Can't I leave you alone for two minutes? Did you just throw them out of the Slice?"

"No, it was nothing like that," I said. I explained to her what had transpired and the reasons behind my actions; it took her a few seconds to consider the implications.

"You're right," she finally said, "but I have a feeling that we're going to have to mend some fences when this is all over."

"Has there ever been a time when we *haven't* had to do that?" I asked.

"No, we do seem to cut a wide swath on occasion, don't we? Anyway, here are two more orders to fill."

"Why are we suddenly so popular?" I asked as I took the slips from Maddy.

"I have no idea, but I don't want to question it. We can use the money, right?"

I laughed. "Always. I'm afraid that we're not going to be able to go over those papers until after

154

work, though. Feel like another sleepover at my place tonight?"

She nodded. "It's the best we can do. I'll go by my apartment on the way to your place and pick up a few things."

"Sounds good," I said as I pulled out more dough to warm as I started making one of the deep-dish pizzas I'd neglected on my menu for so long. I'd started producing them on special order for one customer from up North, but they had caught on and were now a part of my regular menu. "In the meantime, let's make some money."

"You've got it," she said.

Thankfully, the night shift at the pizzeria was without incident, and we managed to keep a good crowd there until the time we closed.

After we cleaned up and sent Josh on his way, Maddy and I locked up and started walking down the promenade toward the shortcut to where our cars were parked. As I turned to look at Maddy, I saw that her gaze was drawn to the crime-scene tape draped near the big bushes by the stage from the show the night before.

"I can't believe that it all just happened yesterday," she said as we neared the shortcut. "It feels like it was weeks ago."

"A lot has happened since then," I said in agreement.

At least we didn't have to walk past the spot where the murder had occurred. I was still staring at it when I saw a flickering light coming from the dense bushes.

"What was that?" I asked as I grabbed my sister's arm.

"What was what?"

"I swear I just saw a light on the other side of those bushes," I said, lowering my voice as I said it.

Maddy looked where I had been staring out for a few seconds before she spoke. "Eleanor, I don't see anything."

"It was there. I swear it was."

"I believe you, Sis," she said as she started in the direction of the crime scene.

"Hang on a second," I said. "Let's think about this. How can this be anything but bad for us if we go back there and find someone involved with Grant's murder?"

"You're not losing your nerve, are you, Sis?" she asked me.

"I don't know. Maybe I am," I said. I truly didn't like the idea of confronting someone who might be a killer in the dark with nothing more than Maddy's bag of defenses, as formidable as the contents of her purse might be.

"Come on," she said and tugged at my arm. I gave in, more because I was curious myself. I knew that if I analyzed our successes in the past as investigators, most of them were due to the fact that we'd forged on when common sense had shouted at us to stop what we were doing and mind our own business.

"It was over here someplace," I said, leading her a little bit away from the direction of the actual tape.

As we approached the bushes, I saw the light flicker again.

Maddy saw it, too, this time.

As we got closer, we were almost off the promenade and into the dense shrubbery, both of us ready to pounce on whoever was there.

Suddenly a car horn honked from the parking lot, and we were both blinded by a pair of headlights pointing straight at us. I heard a rustling sound as whoever we'd been stalking ran away, but I couldn't make out who it was. The figure neared the railroad tracks and then suddenly disappeared into the walking tunnel beneath the rails.

"Blast it! He got away," Maddy said.

"Are we even sure it was a *he*?" I asked.

"No, I couldn't swear to anything about it," she said as she looked toward the car that interrupted our hunt. "Who is that idiot with the headlights and the car horn, anyway?"

As the car crept forward and we got closer, I could see that it was a police cruiser.

That was just great.

Chief Hurley put the car in park, turned off the engine, and got out.

"What were you two doing skulking in the bushes like that?" he asked us. "I didn't figure you two would be crazy enough to go looking at the crime scene after dark."

"We saw someone back there as we were leaving the pizzeria," I said.

"Who was it?" Chief Hurley asked as he reached through his open window and flipped a switch. At once a powerful beam lit up the parking lot, but when he trained it on the bushes, there was no one there. I could have told him that myself, but I doubted that he would have believed me, so it was just as well that he checked for himself.

"I don't see anything," he said as he turned the spotlight off.

"Not after that, you wouldn't," Maddy said. "What were you doing out here tonight? Were you staking out the crime scene, Chief?"

"No, it was nothing like that," he replied a little sheepishly.

"Then why were you hanging out on the promenade?" Then I had a thought. "Chief, you weren't keeping tabs on *us,* were you?" I asked.

He didn't want to admit it, but after a moment he said, "Okay, I confess. Josh asked me to make sure that you both got safely to your cars. Don't tell him I told you. It was supposed to be a secret."

"But he was just here," I said. "Why didn't he walk us out to our cars himself if he was so concerned for our safety?"

The chief grinned. "That's where it gets complicated. He's got a new girlfriend that nobody's sup-posed to know about, and I believe he had a date."

"Josh is dating someone? Who is she?"

"I'm not saying," he answered. "I wouldn't have known anything about it myself if I hadn't spotted him dropping her off at home one night last week. Do me a favor. Don't say anything to him about this, okay?"

"About which part? The fact that you got caught watching out for us, or that you know he has a new girl in his life?"

"I'd greatly appreciate it if you didn't let on about either one of them," the chief said.

"Okay, but what do we get in return?" Maddy asked.

That got the police chief's back up, and for once, I couldn't blame him. I loved my sister more than anything in the world, but sometimes she def-initely had shoe-in-mouth disease. "I'm sorry. Were you under the impression that your discretion counted as something more than a courtesy to me? If that's the way you feel about it, tell my son what-ever you want to. I don't care anymore."

He was about to get back in his squad car when I said, "Hang on a second, Kevin. Of course we won't tell him about any of this. You can trust us."

He shrugged, but at least he stopped retreating, so Maddy added, "I'm sorry for what I said. This whole thing has got me pretty rattled, but I shouldn't try to use your friendship with either one of us against you."

"You're forgiven. Given your situation, I can't say that I blame you a bit," the chief said.

"Are you making any progress?" I asked timidly and then hastily added, "You don't have to answer, but you know that we're dying to find out."

He took a deep breath, ran a hand through his hair, and then said, "It's slow, that's for sure, but we've got a few leads we're pursuing."

I smiled at him. "Chief, we aren't interviewing you for the newspaper. You can be a little more forthcoming than that."

He laughed. "Sorry. I guess I just got a little guarded. I've been burned a few times in the past, though not by you two. I meant it, though. We've got a few irons in the fire going. I've got Chief Hudson from Cow Spots looking into a few things right now for me, too, but he's got his hands full with a mess of his own, so I'm not sure when I'll hear from him."

"What's going on there?" Maddy asked.

"I don't guess it will hurt to tell you. He and the state police just broke up a gambling ring in town. It was being run right under his nose, and Hudson didn't know much about it. He's as mad as I would be, and nobody's going to get away with it if he has a say about it."

"It wasn't at the dry cleaner, was it?" I asked. I based my guess on how Vivian had reacted to us when we pressed her for information, and how she'd folded once she found out that Art Young was in my corner.

160

Chief Hurley looked at me with widened eyes. "How could you possibly know that, Eleanor?"

"It was just a lucky guess," I said.

"I doubt that. Are you sure your buddy Art Young didn't tell you anything about it?"

I was glad that I could answer honestly. "I guess you haven't heard. I haven't talked to him in a while. Our friendship is on the rocks."

"So, you finally wised up and dropped him from your group of friends, did you? That's smart, Eleanor."

I wasn't about to get into that discussion with him.

"We know the woman who runs the place," I said. "Was Vivian arrested, as well?"

"She's in one of my holding cells even as we speak. The chief didn't think she'd be safe in his lockup. How do you happen to know her? It's a little far to take your dry cleaning, isn't it?"

I didn't know how to answer that, so I came up with something else to distract him from pursuing the matter any further. "Grant Whitmore took his dry cleaning to Cow Spots, you know."

"No, as a matter of fact, I didn't," he said. "How did you figure that out?"

I'd done it now. There was no way I could disclose the fact that Maddy and I had done a little B and E, but what else could I say?

Fortunately, I didn't have to. Before I could come up with an answer, the chief's radio squawked. He had a quick conversation with his dispatcher and then got into his car as he said, "We'll have to continue this conversation later, but don't think it's over just because I'm leaving. There was a pileup on the outskirts of town, and they need me on the scene."

He took off with lights flashing, siren wailing, and tires screeching.

"Whew, that was close," Maddy said.

"I think we just delayed answering the question," I said. "Remind me to come up with a good answer for him. Is there any reason to hang around here?"

"Not that I can think of. Whoever was searching the promenade isn't about to come back any time soon."

"Agreed," I said. "Listen, instead of splitting up like we'd planned, I think I'm going to follow you home so you can pack a bag. I've got a weird feeling that something's about to happen, and I don't think we should be splitting up."

"Is it something worse than murder?" she asked me.

"Not necessarily. Just something bad."

"Dear sister, your imagination is in overdrive these days. I'll be fine."

"I know you will," I said stubbornly, "because I'll be right there with you."

"What makes you think that having two of us will help?"

"I don't know it for a fact, but I do know that if I

don't go with you and something happens to you, I'll never be able to forgive myself."

"Okay, tag along, then," she said.

After we got in our separate cars, I followed her through town to her apartment. I watched as she grabbed a few things and threw them all into an overnight bag, but I didn't breathe any easier until we were at my place.

As we walked inside my Craftsman-style bungalow, I waited for Maddy to get over the threshold, and then I firmly latched the heavy oaken door behind us. I didn't realize that I'd been holding my breath, but the second that lock clicked firmly into place, I let out a deep breath.

"You really are spooked, aren't you, Eleanor? I've never seen you like this before, even when we were tracking down killers."

"I don't know what it is. For some reason, this one is just hitting closer to home than the others did. Don't you get the same feeling?"

She thought about it and then nodded. "I guess that I've been fighting it myself, but if I'm being honest with you, I do wonder what's really going on here. Our suspects and allies seem to change with every passing hour, and I'm beginning to wonder who we can trust."

"You can trust me, and I can trust you," I said.

"How about David and Bob? What about Josh, Greg, and Kevin Hurley? Is there any reason we shouldn't trust any of them?"

"No, of course not," I said. "Just ignore me. I'm in one of those moods I get in sometimes. I'm sure that all I need is a good night's sleep."

"That and catching the killer," Maddy added.

"Yes, I admit, that would help make things all better as well. Are we too tired to look at the papers we took from Grant's place? If we are, we could always look at them in the morning."

"I don't think so. I'm wired on adrenaline right now," Maddy said. "Since sleep is out of the question, I say we do a little crime busting."

"Okay then. I'll put on a pot of coffee, and we can get started on the kitchen table. I'm glad we don't own a bakery or a donut shop."

"Why's that?"

"Because I couldn't stand the thought of getting up in a few hours to go to work. I don't know how Paul does it."

"Well, for one thing, he's younger than we are, and for another, he loves to bake, whereas all we really like to do are pizzas."

"Hey, we do other things, too."

"Sure we do, but they're all pizza related. Now, how about that coffee?"

"Yes, Ma'am. Right away, Ma'am."

"That's the spirit," she said with a smile.

As I set up the coffeepot and started brewing the coffee, Maddy grabbed the papers we'd taken from Grant's from her purse and spread them out on the tabletop.

"What's left since we tracked down those telephone numbers?" I asked.

"Oh, there is lots of flotsam and jetsam here," she said as she started pushing the papers around. "There's got to be at least one clue in all of this."

"If there is, it would be great if we can find it."

She drew out the first piece of paper and then said, "Then let's start digging."

Chapter 11

Sadly, after an hour of staring at the same pieces of paper over and over and finishing the entire pot of coffee, we were no closer to a real clue than we'd been before. I was about to put it all away when I spotted something on the floor beneath the table. "What's this?"

I leaned over and picked it up as Maddy explained, "I didn't realize that was down there."

It was a piece of paper covered with random numbers and letters in combinations that didn't make any sense to me at all. Mostly, it looked like an accountant's worst nightmare on tax day.

"What is this supposed to be?" I asked as I studied the paper.

Maddy stared at it for a second and then said, "Funny, I don't remember seeing this. Flip it over."

I did as she asked, and we both saw that this sheet had a list of numbers in an order that at least made some kind of sense.

"The numbers keep increasing as you go along," Maddy said as she looked at it with me.

"Honestly, they almost look like banking amounts," I said. "Do you notice something in particular about these numbers? The increases are always less than ten thousand. These have to be bank deposits."

"That's quite a leap, given the fact that there aren't any dollar signs or decimal places on the paper," Maddy said.

"Maybe so, but if a deposit is over ten thousand dollars, the bank employees have to notify the government. Somebody was trying to fly under the radar here."

"Do you really think that Grant was hiding deposits of this size?" she asked. "There's only one reason he'd do that. He wasn't just trying his best to hide the money from the government. He obviously didn't want *anyone* to find out about what he was up to."

"But where could it all be now?" Maddy asked as she started looking through the rest of the pages we'd taken from his basement apartment. "Eleanor, did you happen to see any checkbooks in his desk, or maybe a stack of deposit slips?"

"There was nothing like that," I said. "The only thing I found related to money was the ten grand I found in the false bottom of his desk drawer."

"But it wasn't ten thousand exactly, was it?"

"No, I put the five hundred you found in with it, and that brought it up to the ten grand count."

"That has to mean that he was getting ready to make another deposit," Maddy said as she looked at the page we'd been studying again. "There's no nine-thousand-five-hundred-dollar deposit listed here," she said, deflated that her theory was off.

"That's probably because he hadn't made the deposit yet."

"So, do you think we're right?"

"Until we can come up with a better theory, for all the good it's going to do us. I suspect that Chief Hurley has the checkbook in his possession, along with all of the deposit slips. He might have already taken the money out himself."

"To keep?" Maddy asked, surprised by what she thought was an accusation.

"Of course not, but that doesn't mean he would want it to be accessible to anyone else. We need to tell him our theory and ask him if we're right."

"Do me a favor. I want to be there when you corner him," Maddy said. "His response will be worth recording on my cell phone."

"You can actually take movies with that thing, too?"

"It's amazing what my little device is capable of. Besides, we both know that we can't go to him with this. It's the same problem we've had before. We can't ask for help unless we're willing to admit what we were doing when we found it, and I wouldn't put it past our chief of police to lock us both up out of pure frustration. And honestly, who could blame him? We probably even deserve it from time to time."

"I don't care what he does. I'm calling him," I said. "There's no way I'll be able to get to sleep not knowing if Grant was hiding all of that money."

"I think you're crazy," Maddy said.

"So, are you saying that you think that I shouldn't call him?"

"Are you kidding? I think it's great that you're even trying. I'm just not sure you're going to be happy with the results."

I dialed the chief's direct cell number, something I'd needed a few times in the past, and he picked up on the second ring.

"Eleanor, shouldn't you be asleep by now?"

"Shouldn't you?" I asked.

"I'm covering tonight for one of my deputies. His wife's in labor, so I told him to go on and take her to the hospital. For the next few days, I'm working double shifts."

"That's awfully sweet of you," I said.

"Sweet nothing. If I made him stay here and work, I couldn't be sure he'd do a thorough job, not that I'd blame him."

"You're not as tough as all that, and we both know it."

The police chief's voice softened as he admitted, "It's a big deal, having a kid. He should be there to enjoy it. Now that we both know why I'm awake, what's on your mind?"

"Maddy and I have been thinking," I said, and I looked up to see my sister stick her tongue out at me. I grinned and continued, "And we were wondering if Grant had any money when he died."

"Why would you ask something like that?" the chief asked.

At least I was ready with an answer this time. "He still owed her money from when they were married, and she's wondering if she'll ever be able to collect any of it now." It was a plausible enough of an excuse, and something that the police chief couldn't easily verify.

At least I hoped that he couldn't.

"Well, she can always file a lien against the estate. I'm sure Bob would be glad to handle it for her."

"But is there any estate at all? Besides the house, I mean."

"I really can't say," the chief said without a moment's hesitation.

"Does that mean you don't know?" I asked.

"No, it means exactly what I said. I can't say."

"That's fine. We'll have Bob check around for any bank accounts he might have in the area tomorrow."

I was about to hang up when the chief said, "Forget it. There's no use keeping it from you, since it's going to be public knowledge soon enough. I found his checking account at his mother's place, and Grant had less than ten bucks in it as of close of business on the day he died."

"Ten bucks? Surely he put more than that away."

"Oh, he did. The only problem is that he didn't keep it in the account. When he closed it out, he took one hundred and fifty thousand dollars out of the bank."

"Where did he deposit it after that?" I asked. "I'm just asking for Maddy's sake."

"As far as we can tell, he didn't stick it anywhere. For some odd reason, he took it all in cash. When he walked out of the bank, he had enough money on him to make some folks think of murder. It was a dangerous stunt to pull, no matter what his reasoning was, and it might just have been what ended up getting him killed."

Chief Hurley yawned and then said, "Keep that under your hat until tomorrow, okay? Somehow a reporter from Charlotte found out about it, and it's going to be in the paper tomorrow morning. Check that. It's after midnight. It'll be in today's paper. Tell Maddy I'm sorry. I'm afraid she's not getting anything out of Grant's estate, but I heard that she was named in the mother's will, so she won't come away from all of this empty-handed, at least not unless Rebecca finds a way to cheat her out of her share. Tell her to keep an eye on that woman. I don't know what it is about her, but I'm not sure that I trust her."

I hung up and then turned to my sister. "Maddy, was Grant a hoarder?"

"You mean like those people I see on television sometimes?"

"No, I mean like someone who would take a hundred and fifty thousand dollars in cash out of the bank and hide it somewhere."

She thought about it for a handful of seconds and then said, "You know, I can totally see that. He never completely trusted banks, and it was nothing to find him with five grand on him as walking-around money, like he used to call it."

"Well, I don't know how he got his hands on a hundred and fifty grand, but nobody knows where it is at the moment."

"Does the chief think he might have been murdered for it?" Maddy asked.

"He thinks it's a possibility, and so do I," I said. "That kind of cash, being untraceable and all, would make him a pretty tempting target for an unscrupulous thief."

"It hurts just thinking about him being killed for his cash," Maddy said. "What if the chief is wrong, though?"

"It's always a possibility. Why? What are you thinking?"

"Eleanor, what if the money is still out there somewhere, just waiting for someone to figure out where it is and take it?"

"What are you suggesting, Maddy? That we go

off on some kind of scavenger hunt? I thought we were searching for Grant's killer, not his cash."

"Of course we are, but if we happen to stumble across the money while we're hunting down a murderer, what are we going to do with it?"

"I've run into something like that before," I said, "and I'll do now what I did then. I'll turn it over to Chief Hurley and let him sort it all out. I haven't missed a night's sleep because of it, and I'm not about to do anything stupid to risk that now. Are we agreed?"

"Absolutely," she said. "It *is* a lot of money, though, isn't it?"

"And that's why there's even more reason to turn it in," I said. "We don't want someone coming after us for it, do we?"

"No, thanks. The two of us have enough problems as it is without adding any more to the mix." She gathered the papers up and then looked at me. "What should we do with these now that we're finished with them? I doubt we're going to get anything else out of them."

"Let's just store them here for now," I said as I lifted up a cushion on the bench of the dining nook. The builders had installed storage areas all over the cottage, and I loved the stowing capacity my little Craftsman-style bungalow had. "When this mess is all over, we can safely get rid of them all, but for the moment, I'd feel better having them nearby, in case we missed something the first few times we looked at them."

Maddy yawned and then said, "I hate to be a party pooper, but I'm really beat. Do you mind if I go on to bed?"

I couldn't remember the last time my sister called it a night before I did, but I wasn't about to crow about it. We'd both had a tough time during the last day and change, but she had the added emotional stress of having her ex-husband murdered near where she lived and worked. It would have been nearly too much for anyone to take, and though Maddy often put on a brave face for the world, I knew that my sister was still feeling the impact of Grant's murder.

"I'm beat myself. I'll see you in the morning, Sis," I said as I double-checked every door and window to be certain we were safely locked in.

"Eleanor, let's just have cereal tomorrow, okay? Nothing fancy, if it's okay with you."

"What's the matter? Don't you like my pancakes anymore?" I asked her with a grin.

"They're perfect, and you know it, but I'd like to get started early. There's a lot of digging we can do before we have to open the Slice for business tomorrow."

"You're okay with us still staying open, aren't you?"

"You bet," she said. "It makes too much sense not to close, but that doesn't mean that I don't want to dig into this more, too."

"Is there anything in particular you have in mind?" I asked as I paused at her bedroom door.

"No, but maybe if we both sleep on it, we'll come up with something."

"Good night, then," I said.

I was afraid that I might have trouble sleeping after all we'd done, and with all the information swirling around in my head, but I dropped off before I even realized it.

Apparently, Maddy wasn't the only one who was exhausted from all that had happened.

"Eleanor, there's someone on your porch," Maddy said the next morning, after I finished washing out our cereal bowls. "Are you expecting anybody to visit this early?"

"No," I said as I shut off the water. "Can you see who it is?"

"Truthfully, I just saw a shadow pass by," she admitted. "But I don't like it."

"I'm sure it's nothing," I said as I walked to the front door. Before I opened it, though, I reached into the hall closet and got out the baseball bat I kept there. I knew that it wouldn't do any good against a gun, but it still made me feel better holding it.

I took a deep breath and then pulled the door open as quickly as I could manage.

Samantha Stout looked startled as I did so, and she was even more surprised by the baseball bat I was holding in my hands. "I'm sorry. I didn't want to disturb you, so when I saw that your sister was here with you, I was planning on just leaving you a note."

"Well, you're here now, and we're finished eating, so why don't you come on in? Would you like a cup of coffee?"

She glanced back at the bat. "That depends. Are you two going to play a game this morning?"

"No, it's just for protection. A girl can't be too careful these days."

"Don't I know it," she said. "If you don't mind, some coffee would be great."

I led her in, stowing the bat back where it belonged along the way. That didn't mean that I trusted the singer any farther than I could throw her, but I sincerely doubted that she was there to physically attack either one of us. If I was wrong, though, I was fairly certain that Maddy had the armaments in her purse to defend us both.

"Hello, Samantha," Maddy said as she handed her a cup of coffee. "I heard you and Eleanor talking, so I got a cup ready for you."

"Why don't we go into the living room, where it's a little more comfortable?" I suggested.

After we were all seated, Samantha said, "First off, I want to apologize for my behavior yesterday at the pizzeria. I reacted badly to your reasonable request, and I'm sorry."

"I have to admit that it was kind of strange of you to refuse a simple request, especially given the fact that you came looking to *us* for help," I said.

"I know. I guess I was so distraught that anyone

could think that I might have killed Grant that it set me off. My ex-husband's reaction was even worse. I can't believe that he just stormed off like that."

"Did you ever catch up with Kenny after you two left the Slice?" I asked.

"Actually, the second I got outside, I decided that it would probably be better if I left him alone, so I took off on my own," Samantha said. "Truth be told, I've been ducking him ever since he stormed out of the Slice like that. The man's got a volatile temper, and honestly, I was more than a little afraid to be around him."

"Has he ever hit you?" Maddy asked gently.

"No, but he's come close more than once. His temper usually only flairs up when he's jealous of another man. I probably shouldn't be telling you this, but he put a guy in the hospital once who was just helping me write a song." Samantha took a sip of coffee, and then she added, "I'm beginning to wonder if he might have had something to do with what happened to Grant after all."

"But you two broke up," I said. "Why would Kenny still be jealous of him?"

"After we split up, Grant was seeing a woman named Vivian Wright in Cow Spots, but he told me that he broke up with her not long after they got together so he could be with me again. I told him that he was insane, and that I'd never date a man who stole money from me, but he wouldn't take no for an answer. The night Grant died, Kenny overheard part of our conversation, and it was all I could do to keep them apart."

"Have you told any of this to the police?" I asked.

She looked scared by the very idea of it. "There's no way I'm incriminating Kenny like that. Who knows what he would do to me then."

"But you're telling us," Maddy said.

"I'm worried that if Kenny thinks you've turned on him, something could happen to the two of you, and I can't have that on my conscience. I came here to warn you both to be very careful around him."

"You have to know that we're going to tell the police everything you just told us, Samantha," I said. "Chief Hurley has a right to know."

"Do what you feel that you must, but I'm trusting you to leave my name out of it. Kenny has to be stopped, but I can't have him realizing that I'm the one who pointed the finger at him. I don't know what he'd do if he found out."

"We'll do what we can to keep your name out of it," Maddy said. It wasn't exactly a promise to keep her identity secret, just a pledge that we would try. I could live with that, but Chief Hurley needed to know about Kenny's wild jealousy.

"You get why we can't make any promises, don't you?" I asked.

"I understand. Anyway, if there's anything I can do, just ask me."

"Where were you when Grant was murdered?" I asked.

"You're still asking me for an alibi, even after what I just told you about my ex-husband?"

"The sooner we can cross you off our list of suspects, the better," I said as reassuringly as I could.

She nodded. "I'm afraid I left the stage after we played a few encores, and then I drove back home, alone. I didn't see anybody along the way or talk to anyone on my cell phone. Honestly, I don't have an alibi, which is one of the reasons I reacted the way I did when you asked me for one."

"I understand," I said. "It's a tough question to have to answer." I didn't think that Samantha's reply meant that she was guilty of anything, but it didn't do anything to clear her name, either.

She put the coffee mug down and then stood up. "Anyway, that's the only reason I came by. Kenny Stout is a liar and a thief, and I'm afraid that he's capable of things much worse than what we've seen so far. Don't believe a word he tells you, and above all else, never turn your back on him."

After Samantha was gone, Maddy turned to me and asked, "What was that visit *really* all about?"

"Don't you believe her story?" I asked.

"I don't know. We both saw a flare-up of Kenny's temper, but that doesn't make anything else Samantha just said true. She did look scared when she talked about him, though."

"I agree. If nothing else, it gives us some food

for thought. I wonder if it's really true that Grant was dating his ex-wife." I couldn't imagine the two of them together, but I'd also seen odder match-ups in my life.

"It should be easy enough to prove one way or the other," Maddy said. "I can't imagine Vivian getting out of jail that fast, can you?"

"How are we going to find out if she is, though? The chief was already suspicious of our connection with her last night. He's not going to let us interview her while she's locked up. You can bet on that."

I grabbed my phone as Maddy asked, "What are you doing?"

"There's only one thing we can do. We need to use the direct approach."

"You're calling the police chief?" Maddy asked as I dialed his cell number.

"There's no better way to find out the truth," I said.

"Hurley," he answered after he picked up.

"Chief, this is Eleanor Swift. Was anyone hurt in the wreck last night?"

"It wasn't as bad as it looked at first. I'm not saying that both cars weren't totaled, but miraculously, everybody got out of it alive. Is that *really* the reason you're calling me?"

"No. I wanted to go ahead and finish the conversation we were having about Cow Spots last night."

"I'd like to do that myself," he said.

"Do you have any interest in coming by the pizzeria before we open today? We can chat then."

"I have a better idea," he said as a car horn honked outside.

"What's that?" I asked, and then I heard the car horn honking again.

"Step out onto your porch and you'll see," he said, and then he hung up on me.

"This is getting to be a habit for you," I said to him when I opened the door and found him standing on the front porch. "You're not stalking me, are you?"

"No, this one's a pure coincidence. I was two streets over when you called, so it was easy enough to swing by here."

"Did you happen to see Samantha Stout as you were driving up?"

"No. What was she doing here?" he asked, clearly surprised by her presence in my neighborhood. "Was it about the murder?"

"So, you know about her connection to the case, then," Maddy said.

"It's immaterial what I know. What have you two been able to find out?"

"She was dating Grant a few months back, but she broke up with him when she lost money in an investment he recommended to her that went bad," I said.

The chief whistled softly as he shook his head. "It doesn't take you two long to get right down to the bone, does it?"

"This murder is tied to us in too many ways," I said. "You knew we'd be digging into it."

"Unofficially, of course I did, but the longer I could ignore your meddling, the better it was for both of us. There's no way around that now, though. Why exactly did Samantha Stout come by here this morning?"

"She wanted to warn us that her ex-husband had a jealous streak even after they separated, and when Grant came by the stage the night he was murdered, evidently things got a little heated between the three of them."

"But he was dating his ex-wife, Vivian Wright, up until the day he died," the chief said stubbornly. "Two sources I checked with confirmed it."

"If you don't believe us, just ask her yourself. She's under your guard still, right?"

He looked angry at the suggestion. "Not anymore. Somebody bailed her out of jail an hour ago."

"Wow, that was fast. How much was her bail set at?" Maddy asked.

"Two hundred thousand dollars, and her boss put it all up in cash," he said.

"No doubt it was from the money he made running a book out of the dry cleaner," Maddy said.

"It goes quite a bit deeper than that. Gambling was just the first bit we've found so far. Who knows how deep it goes?"

I thought about Art Young and the fact that he was in some kind of trouble. He might accept that as a cost of doing business, but it would be hard to lose my friend over a dark rivalry that I knew nothing about.

The police chief asked, "Did Samantha happen to give you an alibi for the time that Grant was murdered?"

"She claimed that she left the stage, got into her car, and drove straight home. Nobody saw her, and she didn't take any cell phone calls, either," I said.

"So then that means that she's not afraid to throw her ex-husband under the bus," Chief Hurley said.

"Maddy and I couldn't tell if she was acting or not, but if she was, she was doing a bang-up job of it. I had the feeling that she was honestly frightened of him when she was here talking about him," I said.

"There could be a great many things that she's afraid of right now," he said. "I need to speak with her, and her ex, as well. Any idea where he might be hiding?"

"I'm sorry to say that I don't have a clue," I admitted, glad that I could answer him truthfully.

"Well, if you see him before I do, tell him that I'm looking for him." Chief Hurley started down the steps but turned to face us before he left. "I'd ask you both to stop digging into this murder, but I hate wasting my breath. If you get in over your head, call me. I don't care what time of day or night it is. Do we understand each other?"

"We do," I said.

As he neared his squad car, I called out, "It's nice to know that you care about us, Chief."

"Well," he said with a slight grin, "Josh loves working at the Slice, and I don't want him to have to go through hunting for another job anytime soon."

Once he was gone, I turned to Maddy. "He likes us. I don't care how much he protests otherwise."

"And who can blame him? We're very likable, as far as I'm concerned," she said.

I glanced at my watch. "We have an hour and a half before we need to go to the Slice. Any ideas about what we might do with our time?"

"I was hoping you'd ask," Maddy said. "As a matter of fact, I do have something in mind at that."

Chapter 12

"So, where exactly am I driving?" I asked my sister as we pulled out of my driveway. "Are we going back to Cow Spots to do some more digging?"

"It does seem as though everyone we're interested in talking to lives there," Maddy agreed. "But what I'd really like to do is get another look at Grant's basement apartment at his mother's house."

"Don't you think that might be kind of risky?" I asked. "We almost got caught the last time we snooped around there."

"What are the odds that Rebecca is going to be there?"

"I'd say that it's a coin toss, if I had to guess."

She brightened at that. "Those are pretty good odds. We'll have some time to snoop if we're lucky."

"And if we aren't?" I asked.

"We can always try to track Vivian down, now that she's out on bail," she answered.

"I think the odds of her being back at Clean Break are close to nothing."

"Then we'll try somewhere else if that doesn't pan out. I wonder how hard it would be to break into Bernie Maine's place?"

I had to laugh at the question. "That's just rhetorical, right?"

She just grinned at me, and I drove to Sharon Whitmore's house to see what else we could find there.

Rebecca's car was parked out front, so that was a dead end for us, at least for the moment. She had a rosebush in a wheelbarrow sitting in the yard, as well as some bagged mulch. "She's planting roses," I said as I drove on past her place. At least she wasn't outside in the yard working when we drove by. I didn't have the slightest idea how we would have explained our presence there, but knowing Maddy, I was sure that my sister would have come up with something just plausible enough to be accepted.

"Should we go to the dry cleaner now?" Maddy asked.

"You're the brains of the operation. I'm just your chauffeur."

"We both know that's a big fat lie," she answered.

I didn't respond and instead just kept driving.

As I'd suspected, the dry cleaner was closed as well.

"That just leaves Bernie Maine's place," Maddy said as I pulled into the parking lot.

"You weren't serious about breaking in, were you?" I asked.

"I'm fresh out of ideas, but if you have any good ones yourself, I'm open to suggestions."

I thought about it, and then I realized that she was probably right. I wasn't all that happy about breaking and entering again somewhere else, but what choice did we have? The longer it took to solve Grant's murder, the worse it would look for every suspect, including Bob, and to a lesser extent, the rest of us.

"Should I park at the welcome center again?" I asked.

"No, let's pull up behind his office. That way no one knows that we're here."

"I'd like to keep it that way if we could," I said.

"You don't have to worry about me, Eleanor. I have no desire to be arrested, either," she said.

"Well, it's good that we agree on something."

* * *

The back door of the office was locked, and on the rare chance that he had hidden a key somewhere else, we checked flowerpots, rocks that looked fake, and even under the doormat.

There was no hidden key, though, at least not one that we could find.

Maddy had leaned over to pick up a big rock when I said, "Hey, I already checked under there."

"The more I think about it, the more this looks like a key to me. After all, what does it do but let people in where they want to go?"

"Well, it keeps people like us out," I suggested, taking the rock from her hand. "Smashing a window would attract too much attention."

Maddy grinned. "*That's* your objection? You've come a long way, Sis. I can remember a time when you'd never bend a rule, let alone break it."

"I admit that I saw the world more as black and white when I was younger, but I'm still not willing to move the line that far back."

"Then this morning has all been for nothing," Maddy said.

"I don't know about that." From where I stood, I could see Bernie Maine's recycling bin, and best of all, it was full of all kinds of discarded papers. "I wonder what we might be able to find in there if we look hard enough."

"Are you willing to dump all of this into the back of your car, because we don't have any trash bags on us," she said.

"Let's just take the recycling bin. We can always bring it back later, after we're finished with it."

"I was right with you until you suggested we return it," Maddy said with a smile.

"I can live with that. I'll get the car door, and you grab the bin."

After it was securely in back, Maddy and I drove out of the driveway.

At least we tried to, but it was kind of tough when Chief Hudson's cruiser was blocking our escape.

Evidently, our presence hadn't gone unnoticed after all.

"Ladies," he said after we parked and got out to talk to him. "What brings you back to our charming little town?"

"I lost an earring the last time we were here," I said. Though I rarely wore jewelry, I was counting on the police chief not to know that.

"Funny, but you're not wearing any now," he said.

"That's because I'm not a pirate. I took the other one off as soon as I noticed that its mate was missing. It's true that I don't wear them that often, but that's what makes them so special."

He clearly didn't believe me, but he evidently didn't know me well enough to come right out and call me a liar. "Did you find it, by any chance?"

"No, I'm afraid it's a lost cause. Just out of curiosity, how did you know that we were here?"

The chief pointed all around us at the businesses and homes interspersed on the block. "They have a decent neighborhood watch around here. Someone called me, so I decided to come over here and check it out for myself."

"Well, then, that's one mystery solved," Maddy said. "Now, if you don't mind moving your cruiser, we're going to be late prepping the pizzeria for our customers today."

"I've never eaten there," he admitted. "Is your food any good?"

"It'll do in a pinch," I said, refusing to be baited by the question.

"Boy, you really know how to sell it, don't you? I'll see you there sometime soon, and that's a promise."

Chief Hudson got into his squad car, and as he did, Maddy reached in back as nonchalantly as she could and covered the recycle bin with a blanket I kept in back.

We waved to him as we drove past, offering smiles we didn't mean.

"Boy, I'm really glad we didn't use that rock," Maddy said.

"I'm happy he didn't look in the back of my car. What would he have said if he'd caught us stealing a recycling bin?"

"Not as much as he would have if we'd broken

into the office. That was a good call there, by the way. Things could have gotten dicey. And the lost earring story? Brilliance, sheer brilliance. I don't know if I've ever been so proud of you in my life."

I thanked her for the compliments, and then I said, "What can I say? I was on a roll." I looked in the back and said, "I'm not looking forward to going through that mess, though."

"Pull over," Maddy said as she pointed to an empty parking lot.

"What's wrong? Did something just happen that I missed?" I asked as I did as I was told.

Maddy got out of the front passenger seat and hopped in back. "I'm going to use our time wisely while you drive. You don't mind, do you?"

"Be my guest," I said. "Let me know if you find anything interesting."

By the time we got to the Slice, Maddy was disgusted. "There was nothing in there that gave me any idea of what Maine has been up to. What a waste of a morning this has turned out to be."

As I parked my car in back of the restaurant, I said, "Maddy, you know as well as I do that most of the leads and ideas we follow up on don't pan out. All we can do is keep swinging and hope we find something that we can use."

"I know," she said as she pulled out the bin. "It's still disappointing. What should I do with this?"

"Just put it by the back door," I said. "We'll deal with it later. Are you sure there was nothing of value to us there?"

"You're welcome to go through it all yourself," she said.

"No, thanks, at least not until I'm really desperate," I said. "For now, let's go get ready to make some pizza."

It was nearly eleven when Paul came by with our sandwich rolls. He made them fresh for us every day at the bakery and gave us a huge discount as well. Usually, it was a bright spot in our day when he came by, but he was clearly distracted by something when he showed up.

"Paul, what's going on?" I asked as he put the bread on the racks we'd installed just for him. "Is something wrong?"

"What? No. I'm fine."

"My dad always used to say that 'fine' was a bad answer to any question but what grit of sandpaper you wanted. Come on. You can talk to us."

Maddy piped in. "Think of us as the sisters you never had."

"Older sisters at that," I said.

"Hey, speak for yourself, Eleanor. If he wants to think of me as his younger sister, I'm not about to try to stop him."

"Maddy, he doesn't need our comedy act. Something is clearly wrong."

"It's nothing," Paul insisted.

"Then tell us about it and let us judge for ourselves. We *are* friends, right?"

"The best I could ask for," Paul answered me. "It's about Gina."

"What about her?" I asked. I knew that they were taking it slow this time around. The two had met in college, but it had fallen apart. When Gina came back to town, they hemmed and hawed before finally deciding to give it another try. I hoped it worked out, but then again, I hated it when any relationship failed.

"We were watching a romantic comedy on TV last night, and I fell asleep," Paul admitted sheepishly.

"It's not the first thing a girl wants to see when she looks over at her boyfriend and expects to see his adoring gaze," Maddy said.

"I understand that, but my hours are so brutal, by eight o'clock I'm completely worn out. It's really not a good excuse, though, because I know that she works just as hard as I do. That hotel can't be easy to run." The hotel in question was quite a bit more than that. Tree-Line was a luxurious complex built on the edge of town that offered a multitude of rooms and had a pretty spectacular convention center as well.

"So, what are you going to do about it?" I asked him.

"I don't know what I can do, but she's not pleased with me. I convinced her to come into town to have an early lunch with me today, but I have no idea how I'm going to make it up to her."

"How early are we talking about here?" I asked.

"Eleven thirty," he replied as he glanced at his watch. "Is any place around here even open then? I'm always grabbing a snack at the bakery, but I can't offer her that."

"Bring her here," I said, suddenly struck by the brilliance of it.

He looked at me a bit oddly. "But you're not even open then."

"We'll make an exception for you," Maddy said, getting into the spirit of things.

"I can't ask you to go to all that trouble for me."

"You didn't ask. We volunteered. Now scat. Bring her by at eleven thirty on the nose, and treat her like she's a princess. And, Paul? Trust us," I said.

"I do," he said. "I don't know why, but I'm already feeling better about everything."

"That's because you know that we won't let you down," Maddy said.

I let Paul back out and then locked the door behind him.

Maddy came out of the kitchen and said, "We've got twenty-six minutes to come up with something spectacular."

"Let me turn on the oven so it will warm up, and then we'll stage something nice out here together."

"What are we going to serve them?" Maddy asked. "Pizza, as good as it is, isn't quite what's called for, for a legitimate apology."

"Don't worry. I'll come up with something," I said.

194

Maddy frowned and then said, "Tell you what. Why don't you take care of the food, and I'll handle things out here."

I really wanted to have a hand in the prep work in the dining room, too, but she was right. I had to get cracking if I was going to come up with something good enough for our special guests.

"Okay, it's a deal. Make it special."

"Right back at you," Maddy said with a grin.

We were in business. I just hoped that whatever we could come up with wouldn't disappoint them.

I started digging through my cookbooks, searching for something really special I could make with the ingredients we had on hand. Thankfully, the pizza dough was finished, so I wouldn't have to use anything that had been refrigerated. Now I just had to figure out what I was going to make. As I flipped through the stack of cookbooks I had, I found and then immediately rejected recipe after recipe that I didn't feel was good enough for the occasion. A quick glance at the clock showed me that I had only eighteen minutes left, though. Just in case my new recipe didn't work out, I made a simple cheese pizza and put it on the conveyor. That way if disaster struck, I'd have *something* to offer them. But it wasn't going to be my lead, if I could help it.

Blast it. Most of the fanciest recipes called for ingredients I didn't have on hand. I was going to have to make do with what I had.

I grabbed more dough, cut some of it into strips,

and then I worked grated Parmesan, mozzarella, and a little cheddar into it all before making a braid, just for fun. I put that on a pan and sent it through the oven and then started on small individual-size dessert pizzas. After I pulled out the cookie crusts that I had made ahead of time and kept on hand, I made one with cherry pie filling and the other with apple pie mix, since I didn't know what they liked. It wasn't nearly as elegant as I would have liked to offer them, but it was the best I could do on such short notice.

At least they wouldn't starve, and I saw that I'd be pulling the first pizza out two minutes after they walked in the door.

I went into the dining room and clapped with delight the second I saw what Maddy had done. She'd pulled all of the tables away from the center of the restaurant until she had one place set apart from all of the rest. Instead of our standard tablecloth, she'd found something that looked elegant in its simplicity. Two new place settings were on the table, and a bud vase in the center held a single red rose.

"How did you do all of this in the time I was in back?" I asked in awe.

"Do you like it?"

"It's amazing," I said. "You've outdone yourself, Sis."

"Thanks. I was going to return the place settings, so I already had them in my trunk, along with some fabric I was thinking about making a new dress out of. It looks stunning as a tablecloth, don't you think?"

"And the rose?" I asked with a grin.

"We were in luck there. I found Hiram Blankenship standing on the promenade, giving them away to whoever wanted one."

"I didn't realize that it was his anniversary already," I said.

"Neither did I, but the man's like clockwork year in and year out."

Every year on the anniversary of his wedding to his late wife, Melissa, Hiram bought twelve dozen red roses and handed them out to everyone he met that day. It was sweet, sad, romantic, and a bit tragic, all rolled up into one act of remembrance that never failed to make me cry.

"You really did great," I said and gave my sister a big hug.

"To be honest with you, it was kind of nice to get my mind off of murder, even if it was only for half an hour. How did you do?"

"Not nearly as well as you did," I admitted.

I was about to tell her what I'd made when there was a tap at the front door. Paul was there with Gina, and he looked so pleased to be with her that I hoped it worked out between them.

"You two shouldn't have gone to this much trouble," Gina said after we shared our hellos and they came into the Slice.

"For two of our dearest friends? It was our pleasure. If you'll be seated, we'll be serving the first course soon," I said.

She turned and looked at Paul. "I still can't believe that you planned all of this just for me."

He was about to confess his part—I could see it in his eyes—so I broke in. "It didn't surprise us one bit. Paul always has had a romantic spirit."

He just laughed, and then he explained, "It's true that I wanted to do something special, but these two ladies deserve all the credit for today."

"It's sweet of all of you, then," Gina said.

I excused myself, pulled the pizza and the cheese sticks out of the line, and then prepped them to serve. As I walked back out, Maddy was getting them sodas, so I served them myself. "I hope you enjoy our humble offerings. Save some room for dessert. I've got cherry and apple dessert pizzas."

"Thank you," Paul said. "I mean it."

"You're most welcome."

Maddy followed me back into the kitchen. "I thought I'd give them some privacy," she said as she opened the door enough to watch them.

I grabbed her apron and pulled her backward away from the door.

"Hey, what if they need something?" she protested.

"I have a hunch that they'll be fine on their own. This is nice, isn't it?"

She nodded. "We should do something like this for our men when things settle down around here."

"Do you ever think that's even a possibility?" I asked.

"I have my hopes. After all, if we can't solve Grant's murder, then surely Chief Hurley can manage to do it without us."

"I hope you're right," I said as I started applying icing to the dessert pizzas. I slid them both back into the fridge, and then I started cleaning up. Maddy lent a hand, and by four till noon, we were ready to face the world.

"Could you go ask them if they're ready for dessert?" I asked.

I didn't have to ask Maddy twice.

She came back fifteen seconds later. "They want both of us out front."

I was curious, so I joined Maddy to find out what was going on.

Paul and Gina were both standing, and I was pleased to see that they were holding hands. "No room for dessert?" I asked.

"We're stuffed," Gina said, and then she hugged me. As she did, she whispered in my ear, "Thanks, Eleanor, for everything."

"It was my pleasure," I said before she broke free.

Paul thanked us, as well, and after they were gone, Maddy and I tackled cleaning up the table and putting everything back into order for our paying customers. She pointed to the cheesy braid of bread and asked, "Did you pull that out of some fancy cookbook?"

"Nope. I take the full blame for it," I admitted. "I made it up on the spot."

"Well, it looks great. I don't suppose there are any more back there, are there?"

"Why don't I make us another batch?" I suggested.

"That sounds wonderful," she said.

Everything was finally back in order, and I had started to unlock the front door when I saw Paul hurrying over to the pizzeria.

I opened the door and asked, "Is something wrong?"

"You need to get inside," he said as he brushed past me and went into the pizzeria. Oh, no. Had something I served them made them sick? I'd hate myself if I ruined their lovely little meal together.

Once I was back in the Slice with Maddy, Paul looked at us both and grinned. "Boy, I never would have believed that it was possible, but you both got me out of the doghouse. That was nothing short of spectacular."

"We're glad you're pleased," I said.

"That doesn't begin to describe it. Now, what do I owe you? I walked out of here on air, and I didn't realize that I forgot to pay you until Gina reminded me a minute ago."

"Thanks for offering, but this one was on the house," I said as Maddy nodded her agreement to my offer.

Paul frowned. "Hang on a second. I never meant you to do all of this for nothing."

"Don't you think we know that, Paul?" I asked as I hugged him. "We meant every word we said. You're like family to Maddy and me. We won't take your money today."

"Okay, but this means that I can bring you treats and confections whenever I feel like it, and you're not allowed to ever say no."

I thought for a split second about protesting when I envisioned what my waistline might end up looking like, but I knew that I had to be careful how I responded.

Fortunately, Maddy filled the silence. "Score," she said to me. "I told you that my little plot would work, Eleanor. Free desserts. Wee!"

"She's just teasing," I told Paul.

"Or am I dead serious?" Maddy asked with a grin.

Paul just shook his head. "If we really were related, I couldn't ask for a better pair of cooks to be kin to."

"We know exactly what you mean," I said. "Now, don't you have a bakery to run?"

"I closed early so I could take Gina out to lunch. There's not much inventory left, anyway, but you're welcome to what I've got."

"Raincheck?" I asked. "We're about to open, so we won't have time to enjoy it."

"Okay, I'll accept that for now, but I'm not giving up."

"I certainly hope not," Maddy said.

After he was gone, my sister looked at me and said, "We did good today, Eleanor."

"We surely did," I said, letting the warmth of good feeling flood through me.

It wasn't very long-lived, though.

When I looked up, I saw Rebecca Whitmore storming toward the Slice, and I doubted that she was in such a rush because she was hungry.

Chapter 13

"I can't believe how reckless you are," Rebecca said the second she spotted Maddy. "Have you completely lost your mind? You're not going to get away with this! Do you hear me?"

"What are you talking about?" my sister asked her. At least there was no one in the restaurant at the moment. I hated it when our personal lives gave our patrons dinner *and* a show, and it happened all too often for my taste.

"Don't play dumb with me, Maddy. You know exactly what I'm talking about. It's gone. All of it. Every last dime," she said.

I thought about the nearly ten thousand dollars that Maddy and I had found in Grant's desk drawer. Had she stumbled upon it herself and then lost it again already? "Slow down, take a deep breath, and think about what you're saying. What exactly is it that's gone, Rebecca?"

"Mother's money, Grant's money, all of it," she said, the anger seething out of her like steam. "There's *nothing* left. You weren't satisfied with a third of Mother's estate, so you made sure that you got all of it, and every bit of Grant's money, too."

"I don't have the slightest idea what you're talking about," Maddy said. "Hang on a second. I suppose that's not strictly true. We *did* just find out that your brother's bank account was emptied out the day he died, but we have no idea what he did with it all, or where he even got it." Maddy looked at me as she realized something. "Eleanor, *that's* where the money must have come from. He emptied the cash out of his mother's estate and put it in his personal account."

"I have to admit that it makes more sense than the blackmail angle we came up with," I agreed.

Rebecca looked confused by our conversation. "Would one of you mind telling me what you two are talking about?"

"We heard that Grant withdrew a hundred and fifty thousand dollars in cash on the day that he died," I explained. "You have every reason to be upset. It's a great deal of money to lose."

"It wasn't lost, it was stolen, and you both know it." Rebecca paused a second and then said, "Wait one second. How much did you say he took out of his account?"

"He cleaned it out completely. From what we've heard, he got one hundred and fifty thousand dollars in cash," I repeated for her.

"You've got to be mistaken," Rebecca said. "My brother never would have done that to me."

"Well, I hate to be the one to tell you, but it looks like you're wrong about that. If anybody stole anything from your mother's estate, my guess is that it was Grant," Maddy said.

"Don't you talk about my brother that way!" Rebecca said as she tried to launch herself at Maddy.

Fortunately, I was close enough to stop her. "Do you want me to call the police chief, or are you going to calm down and get a hold of yourself so we can figure this out?"

"I'm okay," she said after a full minute of deep breathing and, apparently, even deeper thought. "Could it be true? Would Grant really steal from our own mother?"

"Technically, it was most likely from her estate," Maddy said. "Do you have any idea when your mom's accounts were cleaned out?"

"No. I never thought to check," she admitted.

"Call the bank and see," Maddy said.

After a brief conversation, Rebecca hung up her cell phone. "The money in Mom's accounts was transferred the day after she died."

"Where did it end up?" I asked, already knowing the answer.

"In Grant's private account."

"How could he do that legally?" I asked.

"Apparently, he and Mom had a joint account. He had every right to do it, but I know that not a dime of that money was his."

"You're mad at the wrong person," I said. "Maddy didn't do anything wrong."

"I'm not so sure," Rebecca said, clearly searching for some way to absolve her brother of guilt. "Grant never would have been able to do it on his own. You were in on it together from the start, weren't you? Is that why you killed him? For the cash? Where's my money, Maddy? It's rightfully mine."

"Rebecca, you have completely lost your mind," my sister said rather calmly, given the situation and the wild accusations flying around the room.

"Did I lose my mind when I looked out my window this morning and saw you drive by my mother's house? Do you care to deny that, too?"

So, we had been caught, after all. "That was my fault," I said quickly, before Maddy could say anything.

Rebecca looked at me with an acid glare. "Why am I not surprised that you're in on it, too?"

"There are no conspiracies here," I said. The only excuse for our presence that I could come up with was the one I'd used earlier with the chief of police in Cow Spots. "I lost an earring, and I was trying to find it."

"At my mother's house? Were *you* the ones there snooping yesterday?"

Now I was just managing to dig us a hole that

was getting deeper by the second. "Not there. At Bernie Maine's business. He was your brother's business partner, but then you knew that already, didn't you?"

"So what? I know that Bernie wouldn't steal from me."

Maddy butted in. "From what we've heard, he would have tried to steal the president's pants while he was still wearing them. What makes you so special? Have you ever considered the possibility that he's the one who killed your brother and stole all that money?"

"That's pretty cagey, trying to blame someone else for something you probably did yourselves," she said.

"I don't care how it sounds to you. All I know is that you're going to have to leave again. Rebecca, how many times am I going to have to throw you out of my restaurant before you get the hint that you're not welcome here, at least not as long as you continue to accuse us of things we didn't do?"

Rebecca calmed down enough to say, "If you were headed to Cow Spots looking for your earring at Bernie's office, that still doesn't explain why you were at my mother's house."

"It was on the way, and I wanted to see the place one last time," Maddy said. I could swear a tear crept into her eye as she explained, "I just found out about her passing away, and whether you believe me or not, we *were* friends. I admired her, and what's more, I respected her, and I can't say that about many people these days. Your mother was a fine woman, and she'll be missed. I know I've said it before, but I truly am sorry for your loss."

"Well, it turns out that it's your loss, too," Rebecca said, "if what you're telling me is the truth."

"What are you talking about now?" Maddy asked.

"There's nothing left for either one of us to inherit. The house has two mortgages on it, I already told you that her savings and checking accounts are both empty, and she liquidated her retirement money three months ago. Thank goodness she prepaid her funeral expenses and left enough to let me take care of Grant, too. As it is, I'm going to have to take a second job to pay off the seven thousand dollars in bills she still owed." Rebecca started to crack a little, no doubt from the strain of losing her mother and her brother in such a short span of time. I felt sorry for her when I tried to put myself in her shoes, and I couldn't imagine how my sister must have felt.

"Actually, you might not have to do that," Maddy said quietly.

"What do you mean?" Rebecca asked suspiciously.

I tried to warn Maddy off of disclosing the fact that we'd found ten thousand dollars until we were ready to, but she pointedly ignored me. "Do you happen to know if Grant still had that old rolltop desk he used to love?"

"How did you know about that? He had had it since he was a teenager."

"We were married once upon a time, remember? Did you check the lower left-hand drawer, the one with the false bottom?"

"I never knew that it had one," she said.

"I'd advise you to go back to your mom's place and see if anything's tucked away in there," Maddy said. "You might just be surprised by what you find. He always liked to keep some mad money tucked away there for a rainy day."

"I doubt you know what you're talking about, but even if you're right, you're not getting a share of whatever I find. You know that, don't you?"

"I wouldn't take it even if you tried to give it to me. Whatever you find there is all yours," Maddy said.

Rebecca pointed at me. "You heard her say that. You're my witness." She raced out the door, and in a second she was gone.

Maddy turned to me. "Don't even say it, Eleanor. You think I'm a sucker, don't you? You know what? You're probably right. I should have held out for a share of it, anyway."

I touched my sister's shoulder lightly. "You just don't want anyone to know what a good heart you've got, do you?"

"Well, if word got out, I'd hate to ruin my reputation," she said. "There's only one thing that bothers me, though."

"What's that?" I asked.

"What if I was wrong to tell her about the stash of money we found? Did I just give a murderer enough cash to get away?"

"We'll deal with that if it ever becomes an issue," I answered. "Based on what you knew at the time, though, you did the right thing."

"I hope so," Maddy answered.

"Hey, stranger," I said when Greg Hatcher came into the pizzeria's kitchen ten minutes after Rebecca left. "It feels like you've been gone a month."

"It's been barely a week," Greg said as he grinned at me, "but I know what you mean. I've missed this place." Greg was tall and broad, a young man with a good heart, but the thing I loved most about him was his loyalty to the Slice, and to my sister and me.

"So, how bad was the exam? Was it a monster?"

"If it was, I think I managed to tame it," he said. "I understand you've been going through your own set of trials and tribulations. How's Maddy holding up?"

"Didn't you see her when you came in?" I asked. "If she's not waiting on customers, I can't imagine where she might be."

"She's out there, all right, laughing and acting as though no one just murdered her ex-husband. That's the brave face she shows the world, though. I want to know what's really going on with her."

"Honestly, I'm not sure it's even completely sunk

in yet. Right now, she's more concerned about Bob than she is about anything else. He doesn't have an alibi, and what's worse, half the town saw him arguing with Grant the night he was murdered."

"But you two are trying to find the real killer, right?"

"We are," I admitted.

"Have you had any luck so far?" he asked as he put on his apron.

"We've managed to stir things up a bit, but we haven't found the killer yet."

"I hate to ask this, but does your sister have a good alibi for the murder?" He looked so troubled asking the question that I was touched by the display of emotion.

"She was with me the entire time, so I suppose in a very real way, we are covering for each other. Bob was by himself, though, and so was David."

"David? Why would he want to kill Maddy's ex?"

"He wouldn't," I said as I slid a pizza onto the conveyor. "But the police chief still has to consider all of the possibilities, since David was with us, too."

"Well, it should go without saying, but if there's anything I can do to help, don't hesitate to ask. You know that, don't you?"

"I do, but the reminder is always greatly appreciated. Now, you'd better get to work before my sister skins us both. Would you take this to table seven for me?"

"I'm on it," he said.

Before Greg could get away, though, I said quickly, "Hey, I meant what I said. It's good to have you back."

"Believe me, it's wonderful to be here. There's no place I'd rather be."

There was a tap on the kitchen door half an hour later, and then Chief Hurley walked into my kitchen. It was a rare moment when he crossed my threshold, and it was even less likely that he was at A Slice of Delight on a social visit, especially when there was a murderer afoot.

"What can I do for you, Chief?"

"Actually, I'd like to talk to you about something. Do you have a minute?"

"That depends," I said as I made a calzone and put it on a pizza sheet before I sent it through the oven. "I'm kind of jammed this second, but that doesn't mean that we can't talk if you don't mind me working while we do it. What's up?"

"I came by to say that you were right and I was wrong," he said so softly, I nearly missed it.

"Pardon me?" I asked. Did I actually hear what I thought I just heard?

"Eleanor, I won't say it again," he said. "You're going to just have to be content with what you just got."

"I'll try," I said.

"Don't you want to know what it is that I'm talking about?"

"I'm not sure that I care," I said. "Just being right is kind of cool." I hesitated a second, and then I added, "Okay, I have to know. What exactly was I right about?"

"Bernie Maine," he said softly.

"What about him?"

"He's gone."

"Gone? How can he be gone? I thought you were positive that he wouldn't run."

"Hold on. We don't know that for a fact yet. I'm not even sure that he left the area. All I know is that he's not where he's supposed to be. The man just dropped out of sight. I've got my people looking everywhere for him, and Chief Hudson is doing the same in Cow Spots."

"Do you think you'll be able to find him?"

He nodded. "Sooner or later he'll turn up. I'm sure of it."

"That's what you said before, though, wasn't it?" I said. It was unkind, and what's more, I knew it the second it left my lips. "Chief, I'm sorry. I had no business saying anything like that at all."

"It's forgotten," Chief Hurley said.

"Is that all you came to tell me?"

"No, there's something else," he admitted.

I started knuckling the dough into a pan for a classic sausage and pepperoni pizza, and I got too aggressive and shredded the dough instead of kneading it firmly in place. I balled the mess up, stuck it back in the fridge, and got out another ball. "Go on. Tell me," I said.

"We're pretty sure that Maine's armed now," the chief of police said. "We were doing a routine check this morning, and we found out that he's registered two guns under an alias. It took a while to track it all back to him, but there's no reason in the world not to think that he's got both weapons on him right now."

"Why are you telling me this?" I asked, trying my best not to ruin another piece of dough. "You don't think he's going to come after Maddy and me, do you?"

"It's pretty clear that I don't know what he's going to do," the chief said as he ran his hand through his hair. "But he's painfully aware that the two of you are digging into this, and if he *did* kill Grant, he might not appreciate the attention you've been giving him. I heard you were back at his place this morning, and there's probably a pretty good chance that he knows that you were there, too."

So Chief Hudson had ratted us out. I honestly wasn't all that surprised. "It was all perfectly innocent. We were there looking for an earring I lost."

"Eleanor, don't insult me with a story like that," he said with a slight grin to ease the sting of his words. "I know that you have just one pair of earrings you care about, and unless I miss my guess, they're both at home, on your dresser, right now."

"How could you possibly know that? Have you been snooping around my house, checking up on me?"

"I'd never do that without an invitation, certainly not without your knowledge," Chief Hurley said, "but you told me yourself in the past about the way you feel about your earrings. The only pair you care about were an anniversary gift from Joe, and I know that if you really had lost one, you would move heaven and earth to get it back. Am I right?"

"On all counts," I admitted. It amazed me that Chief Hurley had remembered that about me, but then again, he was good at his job, and that included retaining bits and pieces of what a great many different people had told him over the years.

He looked surprised by my admission. "What, you aren't going to try to bluster your way out of it or offer heartfelt denials?"

"Hey, it is what it is. We were there snooping again, plain and simple," I said. "Bernie Maine had a real motive to kill Grant, and right now he's at the top of our list."

"You're talking about Orion."

"I am."

"If you've done your homework, you know that based on that, Bernie wasn't the only one with a motive to kill Grant, then."

"Don't worry. Samantha and Kenny Stout are both on our list, too."

The chief didn't react when I asked him to move so I could retrieve a pizza sub that was just coming out of the oven.

As I cut it, Greg came back. "Is that one mine?"

"No. This is Maddy's. Yours is next, though."

"I'll take it for her, and then I'll be right back," he said before he disappeared.

"Sorry to bother you here, Eleanor. I can see that you're busy, but I thought you should know," the chief said and started to leave.

"It's under control. You're fine. You don't have to leave." I didn't want him to go, not when he was in the mood to share information with me. Who knew how long it might be before he felt that way again?

"Have you had a chance to talk to Kenny Stout yourself?" I asked, remembering how Samantha had shivered in fear the last time I heard her say his name.

"I have," he admitted. "But I really don't see him having any real motive here. Whatever Samantha has been up to, it happened when the two of them were separated, and Kenny told me that he didn't have any of his own money invested with Maine himself."

"It goes a lot deeper than that, at least as far as what Samantha told us today," I said as I cut the next sandwich in line, plated it, and put it on the table for Greg to pick up.

"What I still don't get is why she even came to you in the first place this morning," the chief said. "What did she think you two would be able to do?"

"Actually, that wasn't the first time she reached out to us," I said. "She and Kenny both came here yesterday to enlist our help."

"Help with what?" he asked, clearly intrigued now.

Greg came in, grabbed the sandwich, and then left without a word.

"They were afraid they were going to be railroaded into an arrest and a conviction if they didn't do anything to protect themselves."

He looked grim as he said, "Eleanor, I wouldn't take part in that. Not ever."

"Everyone knows that," I said, "but Maddy and I were hoping we would get alibis from them and eliminate them as suspects. We both know that turned out to be a bust. We never even got Kenny's alibi, and we already told you that Samantha's is basically nonexistent."

"If it's any consolation, Kenny's isn't any better," the police chief said. "They both admit that they took separate cars from the fair, and neither one of them has a single person vouching for their whereabouts. You were telling me about your conversation with Samantha Stout before. What was your overall impression of her?"

"Well, she's afraid of her ex-husband. Kenny's got a temper, something I've seen for myself, and he hated Grant with a real passion."

"You say that you saw him upset, but what about the rest of it?"

"What about it?" I asked.

"Do you have any other evidence that Samantha has a reason to be afraid of Kenny other than what she told you? I've looked into it, and there have never been any police reports filed on either one of them. As far as I can determine, she's never shown up at the hospital with bumps and bruises, either. Has anyone actually ever heard him threaten her?"

"Just because she might not have proof doesn't mean that it never happened," I said, doing my best to keep my own temper in check.

"I understand that," Chief Hurley said softly. "For all I know, everything she told you is true. There's just nothing to back it up."

"You know what? You're right. There's a chance that I could be all wrong about her," I admitted. "There's no way to prove it at this point one way or the other."

To the chief's credit, he didn't gloat when I made the admission. "As long as we're both keeping our minds open to the possibilities, we'll both be better off."

"Speaking of which, I think I should come clean with you." I was going to share some of what we uncovered, but not tell him how we'd attained the information. I wasn't that crazy. "We have four suspects on our list. Would you like to hear who they are and why?"

He looked around the small kitchen. "You're not recording this, are you?"

"Of course not," I said.

"I know. I was just teasing you, Eleanor. In all fairness, I'm not necessarily going to tell you anything else about the case, no matter what you say to me. You know that, don't you?"

"I don't expect anything, but I'll take whatever you can give me," I said.

"Then go ahead."

"Okay, here we go. I'll give you the names first and then why we suspect them. It would be great if you could tell me if I was off base on any of them."

"We'll see," he said.

I was about to start when Maddy came into the kitchen with three more orders. "Are you still here?" she asked Chief Hurley with a grin.

"Sometimes you just can't get rid of me," he answered sociably enough.

Maddy turned back to me. "Is that pizza ready?"

"One second," I said as I watched it pass the center point of the exit line, the place where I considered it safe to pull any pizza or sandwich from the conveyor. I knew that sometimes when Maddy ran the kitchen, she pushed that line back a little no matter how much I protested, but I wasn't about to say anything about it now. I pulled the pizza, panned it, and cut it, and as Maddy took it, she winked at me without saying another word to Chief Hurley.

"Okay, let's try that again," he said.

"We've got Rebecca Whitmore first on our list. She may or may not have known that her brother had basically stolen her entire inheritance out from under her, but if she did, it could have made her mad enough to kill him. Next in line we have Samantha Stout. Not only did Grant lose her money, but he also started dating his ex-wife, Vivian Wright, the dry cleaner they just arrested in Cow Spots, the second they broke up. We know that Samantha claims she dumped Grant and he begged her to take him back, but we don't have anybody's word but hers for that. Next, we've got her ex, Kenny. As I said, he was jealous, maybe even enough to kill Grant if he saw him as a threat."

"Are you saying that he still wants Samantha back?" the chief asked.

"I'm not, but she might think so. Then again, it may be a case where he doesn't want anyone to have her if he can't."

"Go on."

"We've also got Bernie Maine on our list, for the obvious reason that Grant might have scammed him. From what I've seen, Bernie doesn't seem like a man who takes to being trifled with."

"He's not. Is that it?"

"We have one more suspect on our list. Last but not least, there's Vivian, the dry cleaner. If Grant dumped his ex-wife, it's not hard to believe that she could have been mad enough to kill him out of anger."

"Eleanor, are you and Maddy comfortable with your list of suspects as being final?"

"Not particularly," I admitted. "That's why we're still digging."

"I get that," Chief Hurley said, "but don't take

any chances, especially with Bernie Maine. If you see him, get away from the guy as fast as you can and call me. He's not playing around, Eleanor, and neither should you."

"Is there anything that *you* would like to share? What's your suspect list look like?"

"I have a few more names on mine than you do," he explained a little reluctantly. "You're not going to ask me who they are, are you?"

Who had we missed? Was there someone else in Grant's life we hadn't uncovered yet? And then I knew. Bob Lemon was on it, and most likely, David had a mention as well. I was about to defend them both yet again, but I decided that for the moment, it would be in my best interests to keep getting along with our chief of police.

"No, I have a hunch that I already know."

"That's that, then," Chief Hurley said when he realized that I wasn't going to add anything else to the conversation. Did he look a little disappointed by my reticence? Perhaps he'd been hoping I'd complain enough that he'd be justified in cutting me out of the loop. If that was the plan, it was going to fail miserably.

After he was gone, Maddy came back into the kitchen in ten seconds. "Tell me everything."

"Don't you have customers out there?"

She shrugged. "Greg's got things under control. Now spill."

"Okay, but it's going to be fast and dirty."

After I quickly brought her up to speed about

my conversation with the chief of police, my sister nodded. "It's mostly what we expected, isn't it?"

"All except the fact that Bernie Maine is on the loose with at least two weapons, and maybe more."

Maddy bit her lower lip. "There's that, all right. Do you have any idea what we should do during our lunch break?"

"To be honest with you, I'd just as soon stay here, make something fattening to eat, and try to forget about this entire mess for an hour. I don't know who else to talk to at this point, or what I could say to them if I could come up with a name."

"You're not getting discouraged investigating Grant's murder already, are you?" Maddy asked.

"Maybe a little bit, but you know that you don't have to worry about me quitting on you. I'm not giving up until we find the killer. I guess I'd just like a little break from it all, though."

"Then that's what we'll do. We'll have our own little party here at the Slice," Maddy said with a smile. "We can even invite Greg to stay behind with us and make it a real feast. If you'd like, I can call Bob and David, as well."

"Are you sure that you don't mind that we're not digging during every free second we have?" I asked. It had to be a sacrifice giving up even a minute of time that we could spend investigating, and I knew it couldn't be easy on her.

"Absolutely. Who knows? Maybe a bit of a break will give us a fresh perspective, and we can look at all of this a little clearer than we're seeing it right now."

"I appreciate that." I hugged Maddy. "Thanks, little sister."

"You're very welcome, big sister," she said in return.

Chapter 14

"That was wonderful," I said to Maddy just after we kicked the men in our lives out the front door and locked it again.

"The food or the company?" she asked.

"Both," I replied.

Bob and David had happily come over to the Slice to spend some time with us, though Greg had excused himself, saying that he had errands to run. I thought it might be because he didn't want to be the fifth wheel, and I wondered if there were any young women he was interested in at the college. It was probably hard on him, knowing that his best friend, Josh, had a new girl in his life, and I was afraid that Greg might be lonely. If I thought hard enough about it, I might just be able to . . . I stopped myself right there. I'd butted into the poor young man's life enough in the past. There was no need for me to keep at it. He was perfectly capable of getting a girlfriend without my meddling.

"Those two can be a load of fun when they want to, can't they?" Maddy asked as we started cleaning up our plates and glasses. "I'm thrilled about how small we kept the talk. Did you notice that neither one of them asked us about our investigation?"

"It was just what I needed. Thank you for not bringing it up, either."

"Hey, I needed a bit of a break just as much as you did." As we finished cleaning off our table, Greg knocked on the front door.

After Maddy let him in, he surveyed the dining room. "You must have done a good job, because I don't see any signs of it myself."

"Signs of what?" Maddy asked him.

"The wild party that you two just hosted," he said with a grin.

"Oh, we've learned to keep that to a minimum," I said.

"It must be one of the benefits of getting older," Greg replied with a smile.

"Watch it, buster," Maddy said as she flipped her wash towel at him. "You'll be our age before you know it."

"That's nothing but lies, rumors, and false-hoods," he said as he grabbed his apron. "I'm going to be like Peter Pan myself; I'm never growing up."

"Sorry, but it's too late for that. You already did," she said as she stuck her tongue out at him.

Thankfully, it was a quiet evening at the Slice, and by the time we were ready to close for the night, I was all set to go home, take a hot shower, and read a little before I fell asleep. Maddy was still bunking with me, though, so it was hard to say what our evening would really end up like.

Maddy and I were standing outside at the front door of the Slice and locking the place up ten minutes after Greg had left when someone came hurrying toward us out of the shadows.

I just had enough time to get my sister's attention and turn her around to face the onrusher with me, but there was really nothing else I could do.

"Where's my wife?" Kenny Stout demanded angrily when he reached us.

"We have no idea where Samantha might be. Why are you so upset about it? I thought you two were finished," I answered as calmly as I could manage. Maddy was slowly reaching into her bag, so I needed to distract Kenny long enough to give her time to take something out of the bag of defenses she called a purse.

"Don't try to get cute with me, Eleanor. I'm not

in the mood for it. Tell me where she is, and I'll leave you two alone."

"Like I said, we don't know where she is, but even if we did, I doubt that we'd tell you while you're shouting at us," I said.

He shook his head in disgust. "You women all stick together like you're in some kind of a club. I just want to see her."

"Well, she clearly doesn't want to see you. Doesn't that tell you anything?" I asked.

"What did she say to you?" he asked angrily. "Did she tell you that I was abusive toward her or some kind of nonsense like that? The woman's an artist. She exaggerates everything that comes out of her mouth."

"Well, she *was* pretty convincing when she came by my house this morning," I said.

Maddy finally pulled something out of her purse and pointed it at Kenny. It was her stun gun, and for once, I was glad she always had it on her. "Back off, Kenny. I don't want to hit you with this, but I will if you push me."

Kenny looked at Maddy, took one step forward, and then casually jerked the weapon out of her hand. "Don't point something dangerous at someone and then warn them about what you're going to do," he said. "What if I really were a bad guy, instead of a man just looking for his estranged wife?"

"Give that back to me," Maddy demanded. She

looked shaken by how easily Kenny had disarmed her.

"You'll get it when we're finished here," he said, "and not a second sooner."

"I already told you," I said. "We honestly don't know where Samantha is."

That was when Kenny took another step toward Maddy.

"Don't shoot her with that!" I commanded.

"I wasn't going to," Kenny said. He offered the stun gun to Maddy, who took it and jammed it back into her bag.

In a softer voice, he said, "Contrary to what Samantha must have told you, I'm not some kind of monster. Go on. You can go."

Kenny stood there as we walked away, and I held my breath until we made it around the corner.

The second we did, I turned to my sister. "Maddy, are you okay?"

"No, I'm not, not even one little bit," she said. "Can we leave my car here tonight? I want to ride back with you."

"Of course we can," I said. I put my arm around her shoulders and felt the rigidity of her body next to mine. "Maddy, I couldn't believe how fast he was when he grabbed that stun gun. He would have taken it from anyone."

"But he didn't, did he? He took it from me like I was some kind of spoiled child with a toy. Eleanor, I've been putting my faith in my purse arsenal all these years, but I can see now that I was wrong to do it."

"You can't beat yourself up about what just happened," I said as we got into my car and headed to my house.

Maddy was shaken more than I even realized.

We drove in silence, and neither one of us was completely at ease until we were inside my place with all the doors and windows locked.

"He was right, you know," Maddy finally said softly as I made us both some tea.

"About what?"

"I shouldn't have warned him first. We felt threatened, and I should have zapped him when I had the chance. Worse yet, I saw him reaching for the stun gun, and I just stood there and let him take it from me like I was some kind of helpless fool. It's not going to happen again. I can promise you that."

"It turned out okay, though. He wasn't trying to hurt us," I said.

"But he could have had something a lot darker in mind than trying to get information out of us," she answered. "In a way, Kenny did me a favor. He hurt my pride, but he taught me an important lesson by doing it."

"Can we just drop it and change the subject?" I asked as I handed her a mug.

"What do you want to talk about? Samantha?"

I shuddered a little as I said, "She has a reason to be afraid of him, doesn't she?"

"I'm not so sure," Maddy said.

"How can you say that after what just happened?" I asked my sister after I took a sip of tea. Its warmth was welcome after the chill I'd experienced outside the Slice earlier.

"He was clearly agitated with Samantha and the two of us, but when he had us in a vulnerable position, his first reaction was to give my stun gun back to me. I'm not so sure that Kenny's a bad guy, after all."

"Sure, he didn't stun us both, but I'm not so sure that makes him okay in my book. As a matter of fact, I'm going to keep my eye on him more than ever."

"You do that," Maddy said. "Where do you think Samantha is hiding?"

"If she has any sense, she's long gone," I said. "We can't plan on ever having the chance to talk to her again. We're going to need to come up with another angle to pursue."

After taking a sip of her tea, Maddy said, "I think we should try to track Vivian down tomorrow before we open the Slice. She could very well hold the key to the whole thing. Hopefully, that part of her life has settled down enough for us to get a reasonable answer from her, thanks to Art." When I didn't reply, she asked, "You're worried about him, aren't you?"

"I am, but for more reasons than that, though."

"I still don't get the friendship you two share, but I know that it's genuine. If you're that worried about him, why don't you call him?"

"He asked me not to, and to be honest with you, I'm not even sure the number I have for him will work anymore," I said.

Maddy looked at me for twenty seconds and then asked, "Are you just saying that because of what you're afraid you'll hear? If he's in trouble, and he's the friend you say he is, you should call him."

I thought about it and then nodded. "You're right. The least I can do is try."

I took out the number I had for Art and dialed it.

To my surprise, Art himself answered.

"Is that you?" I asked.

"Eleanor, how did you know that I was just about to call you?" He sounded genuinely puzzled by my call.

"I'm sorry. I know that you've got a lot of things going on in your life right now and I'm not supposed to contact you, but I've been worried about you." I just got what he'd said, so I asked, "Why were you going to call me?"

"Everything has been taken care of," Art said, the relief clear in his voice. "Our friendship is in full force again, if you're interested. Feel free to speak with Vivian Wright, or anyone else you'd like to grill. The storm has passed."

It was great news; there was no doubt about that. "Wow, that was fast. Does that mean you're coming back to Timber Ridge?"

"In due time, but right now I have a friend who needs me on the West Coast, so I'm flying out tonight to see if I can lend him some aid."

"What kind of help are you giving him?" I asked him, afraid that he might give me an answer that I didn't want to hear.

"His wife just died of cancer, and he needs me with him. I'll be back in a week, and when I do get back to Timber Ridge, I'd love one of your pizzas."

"You know that all you have to do is ask," I said. "Have a safe flight, and tell your friend I'm sorry for his loss."

"I will do just that. Good night, Eleanor. It was good talking to you."

"You too. Good night," I said.

"What was that all about?" Maddy asked me as I put my phone back down on the kitchen counter.

I thought about explaining to her what Art had shared with me, just to make sure that she realized that there was more to my friend than she could ever know, but then I decided that it was something that would be better just between the two of us. "We got the all-clear sign to talk to Vivian."

"He's okay, then?" Maddy asked me softly.

"He's just fine. Thanks for asking," I said.

"Hey, no matter what, you're my sister. I don't have to like everyone you do, but I'm such a big fan of yours that I'm inclined to, anyway. I was going to confront her tomorrow, anyway, but I'm glad that we got the green light to talk to her from Art. What are the odds we're going to be able to track her down, though?"

"Hang on a second," I said as I dug out my telephone book. I found the dry cleaner's number at the shop, dialed it, and listened to the machine as it gave me the shop hours and the day's special. "They're still open."

"Unless they forgot to change the outgoing message on their machine before all of this happened," Maddy said.

"There's only one way to find out, isn't there? We need to head back to Cow Spots in the morning and see if we can get anything out of Vivian."

"We've been there so much lately, I'm thinking about looking for an apartment."

"You're kidding, right?" I asked. I loved having my sister so close, and the thought of her living somewhere else, even if it was just the next town over, was too much for me to take. Apparently, I leaned on her more than I'd realized.

"Don't worry. I was just kidding. Can you imagine ordering the return address labels? Timber Ridge is bad enough, but Cow Spots is just an open invitation for ridicule."

"I don't know. I think it's kind of cute."

"Well, you can't move, either."

I touched a nearby wooden column, carefully

restored during our rehab. "Sis, we both know that I could never leave this place. There's too much of Joe in it."

"Even if you and David got married somewhere down the road?" she asked. "Would you still live here?"

"It's my home," I said.

"I'm not saying that it's even on the horizon, but let's play what-if for a second. Do you think David could live here, what with Joe's ghost around every corner?"

"Joe isn't haunting me," I said.

"Not now he's not, but then again, David's not here now, either."

"Maddy, if there's one thing I'm certain of, it's that Joe would approve of me moving on with my life. He loved his life too much to deny anyone else happiness if they had a shot at it."

"He was a pretty special fella, wasn't he?" she asked.

"Golden," I said as I yawned. "I don't know about you, but I'm beat."

"You never really answered my question, though, did you?" she asked as I walked toward the master bedroom.

"Didn't I?" I replied with a grin.

As I got ready for bed, I realized that the reason I'd avoided Maddy's question was that I didn't know what the answer was. Could I invite someone else into the home that Joe and I had created together? Or, even worse, could I leave this place in order to live with someone else? I honestly didn't know, and since David wasn't about to propose and I knew that *I* wasn't going to do it, I was pretty safe just ignoring it for the moment. I planned to enjoy my relationship with David for as long as I could, and if it eventually grew into something deeper, I'd make that decision then.

"Can I help you?" Vivian asked as we walked into the Clean Break the next morning. She didn't even look up from her newspaper to see who was in her shop.

"I'm glad to see that you're out of jail so fast," I said brightly.

No one else was around, but as she looked up at me, she said urgently, "Would you keep your voice down? How did you know about that?"

"It's not supposed to be some kind of big secret, is it?" Maddy asked. "If it is, you've got a problem. We found out an hour after you were arrested. How long do you think it's going to take the citizens of Cow Spots to find out? If they're anything like the people who live in Timber Ridge, it's already common knowledge around here."

"It was all just a misunderstanding," Vivian said.

"Really? Is that how you're going to try to spin it? Vivian, you were booked for soliciting gambling and released on a higher bail than I could have scraped together in a year. That doesn't sound like a misunderstanding to me," Maddy said.

"My employer has hired an attorney for me," she said. "Once he's got this all straightened out, it's not going to matter."

"Don't kid yourself," Maddy said. "Even if they did try to forget about it, a new murder charge will remind them pretty quickly."

"I didn't kill anyone," she said flatly.

"Hey, I can understand it," I said. "It couldn't have felt good when Grant dumped you like that and decided to chase back after his old girlfriend."

"Do you honestly think that he'd dump me for a run-down old hag like you?" she asked Maddy.

My sister didn't blow up, which might not have been a good sign, but I was going to pretend for the moment that it was. Instead, she said, "We weren't talking about me. Besides, I was *married* to him too, remember? Why on earth would I want to have leftovers after I didn't really enjoy the meal in the first place?"

"Who are you talking about, then?" she asked petulantly.

"Samantha Stout," I supplied.

"There was no way that was going to happen, either. Grant told me he was done with her when she lost her faith in his money-managing skills."

Now, that was a spin if I'd ever heard one. "He stole from her, Vivian, and then he begged Samantha to take him back, but she wouldn't do it. How's that fit into your skewed little view of the world now?"

"Grant was cheated right along with everybody else," Vivian said. "Bernie Maine took it all himself and then blamed Grant for it so people wouldn't lynch him instead."

Was there any chance that had a hint of truth in it? If I hadn't heard Chief Hurley's story about Grant's massive bank account withdrawal, I might have even believed it myself. "Then why did Grant suddenly have so much in his bank account, and more importantly, where did it go?"

"What are you talking about?" she asked. "Grant was extremely well off. He always had been."

"Is that what he told you?" Maddy asked her. There was more than a hint of condescension in my sister's voice, but I couldn't blame her. After all, Vivian had already taken a fair number of shots at my sister. "And you believed him? You poor thing."

"He showed me his checking account," Vivian said triumphantly.

"How hard could that be to fake?" I asked.

"And a bank statement, too," she added.

"We're not saying that the money wasn't there at one point. The fact is, he pulled every last dime out of his account right before he died, and now it's all disappeared."

"He scammed me," Vivian said with a hiss, the air deflating out of her. "I can't believe it. What a jerk he was, and what an idiot I was for believing him twice."

"If it's any consolation, he fooled more women than you, and that includes me," Maddy said, softening toward the woman suddenly. My sister was a mass of conflicting actions and beliefs, but I knew that in the core of her heart, she cared about other people, no matter how much she protested at times that she didn't.

"Vivian, is there a chance he gambled the money away before he died?" I asked. "We found a slip in an envelope from the dry cleaner."

"Sure, maybe twenty bucks on a pony that couldn't run, but nothing over that," she said, and then Vivian realized just what she was admitting to us. "I take that back. I'm not admitting that I ever did anything but take in laundry here," she added quickly.

"Understood," Maddy said, "but how can you be so certain he didn't just bet it all away with someone else?"

"Nobody around here could cover that kind of bet, especially without me knowing about it. But none of that matters. Grant quit gambling after he crossed the wrong guys in Vegas last year. They made a very convincing argument, and he was afraid to flip a coin after that. Or didn't you know about what happened there?"

"Thankfully, our ex-husband didn't share his

later adventures with me," Maddy said. "How sure are you that he wouldn't gamble?"

"As sure as I can be," she said.

"So, if he didn't gamble it away, where did it all go?" I asked. "A hundred and fifty thousand dollars doesn't just vanish into thin air."

"You'd be surprised by how fast someone could spend it if they were determined enough to do it," Vivian said.

"That sounds like the voice of experience," I said.

She shook her head. "The most I've ever had at one time to blow was three thousand dollars. Granted, I went through it pretty quick myself, but it was bush league compared to what some folks have done." She paused and then added, "Listen, I was told to cooperate with the two of you if you ever came back, but there's nothing more to tell, and that's the honest truth."

"Vivian, we need to contact your alibi," I said, "and the exact times you were together. If everything checks out, we'll promise to leave you both alone."

"I can't tell you where he is," she said. "I'm really sorry. I wish I could, but I can't."

"Then I'm afraid we aren't finished here yet," Maddy said. There was an edge of determination in her voice that was unmistakable.

"Hang on," she said and then dialed a number.

"I need more instructions," was all that she said. After a moment, she whispered into the phone, waited, and then spoke again. The next second, she was handing the telephone to Maddy.

My sister took it and said, "Hello?" After a pause, she added, "No. One second."

She thrust the telephone at me. "He wants to talk to you."

I took it from her, identified myself, and then listened.

"Vivian was with me from six to eleven fifteen the night Grant Whitmore was murdered."

"No offense, but why should I believe you? I don't even know who this is."

"You might not, but we have a mutual acquaintance, and I promised him on my mother's eyes that I'd tell you the truth. If you don't believe me, then I guess you'll just have to believe him. We both know that it would be foolish for me to lie to you at this point."

For some reason, I believed him. It was nothing I could take to Chief Hurley, and now, more than ever, I was determined not to even mention it to him.

"Thank you," I said.

"You're welcome."

I handed the phone back to Vivian and then turned to Maddy. "Come on. We're leaving."

"Are you sure?" she asked me, still staring at Vivian.

"I'm positive. Whoever was on the other end of

the line might not have a problem lying to me or even the police, but I know that he would never mislead my friend."

"Okay. Got it."

When we left Vivian, I could swear there was a look of respect in her eyes, as if the fact that my connections were deeper than hers gave me something in her eyes. It was not something I wanted, but it had been useful, and I hadn't regretted using it.

At least Maddy and I could strike one name off of our list of suspects, and that was real progress in my mind.

Chapter 15

As I drove back to Timber Ridge, Maddy asked me, "Who do you think killed Grant, Eleanor? Don't try to tell me that you don't have any idea, because I know you better than that. You've got to have come to some conclusions by now."

I thought about her question for nearly a minute before I answered her. "Maddy, it's like asking a mother of twelve who her favorite child is. Who knows? They might even have one, but I doubt they'd ever admit it out loud. If I guess right now, there's a nearly certain chance that I'd be wrong. How about you?"

"I was hoping you had something more than I did," she admitted. "What's going on with us? We usually have a lot more luck with these cases than we seem to be having right now. Or is it just me?"

"I guess that it's still just too early to say. You've got to remember that Grant has only been dead a few days. Most likely, it's going to take quite a bit longer before we figure this out, if we ever do."

"Don't even think that," Maddy said, the angst in her voice coming through loud and clear. "I don't know how Bob is going to handle this if the killer isn't caught soon."

"Has he said anything to you about how this is affecting him?" I asked her.

"He called me last night on my cell phone after we went to bed. He was troubled by all of this and wanted to talk, and I was up half the night with him trying to calm him down."

"You didn't say anything to me about it this morning," I said.

"Bob asked me not to, and since it concerned him, I didn't see how I could refuse the request, you know?"

"But aren't you breaking that right now by telling me about it?"

"He knows that when my promises concerning you are the subject, he'll be lucky to get an hour of silence out of me."

"If that," I said with a slight grin.

"What can I say? I tell my sister everything."

"And your sister appreciates that," I said. "How bad is it?"

"He's considering packing up his practice and moving somewhere else if things don't get better soon," she explained.

"Is he serious? Does that mean that you'd go with him?" I couldn't stand the thought of Maddy leaving Timber Ridge. Not having her in my life would make my existence a pretty bland experience all in all.

"I don't even want to think about it right now. Let's just hope it doesn't come to that," she said.

That was not the answer I'd been hoping to get. I had to let it go, though. "Then we need to work harder at finding the killer, and fast."

"What more can we do that we haven't already done?" she asked, the exasperation clear in her voice.

"We need to keep digging, keep poking around, and get as many people off balance as we can," I said. "Somebody's bound to snap."

"That sounds like a recipe for our own lynch mob," Maddy said with a smile.

"Hey, I'm willing to do whatever it takes to drive the killer out into the open," I said.

I was about to say something else when I glanced in my rearview mirror and saw a black BMW following us five or six cars back. "You are not going to believe this."

"What's happening?"

"Don't look behind us, but I think I just found Bernie Maine."

"Are you kidding?" Maddy asked. She started to turn in her seat, but I put a hand on her shoulder.

"What did I just ask you? If you have to look, use the vanity mirror on your visor."

She did as I requested and then slowly nodded in agreement. "It's Bernie, all right, unless somebody else is driving his car. What's he doing following us?"

"I don't have a clue. If he's tailing us, he must be lost. Could he honestly believe that we're a threat to him?"

"He must. Why else would he risk being caught following us? That's not exactly an inconspicuous car he's driving. What are we going to do?"

I had taken my phone out and had put it on the dash between us. "I'm going to call Chief Hurley," I said.

"He'll see you making a call, and we can't afford to spook him," she said. "Let me do it."

"Go on, then. Grab my phone and try to get him," I instructed her. "He's on my contact list."

"I can use my phone. He's on my list, too," she said. That was news to me. Perhaps my sister was getting a little more prudent as she got older. Having the chief of police's number on automatic dial meant that at least she was finally beginning to realize that we couldn't handle every situation by ourselves. I never would have believed it if Maddy hadn't told me herself.

She put her phone on speaker so we could both talk to the chief of police.

When he picked up, I said, "Chief, this is Eleanor."

"Am I on speaker? I hate speakerphones. You know that."

"Sorry if it's inconvenient, but I thought you might like to know that someone is following us. Maddy and I just noticed him four cars back, and I doubt that he realizes that we're onto him. Care for a guess about who it might be?"

"It's not Bernie Maine, is it?" he asked.

"It is indeed, or at least his car," Maddy said.

"Don't do anything, Eleanor," the chief said.

"If I stop driving, he's going to rear-end me," I said.

"You know what I mean. What I should have said was, 'Don't do anything different.' Where are you right now?"

"We're on two-fifty-eight, between Cow Spots and Timber Ridge."

"In which direction are you traveling, and which town are you closest to?"

I looked at Maddy and asked, "We're about ten miles from Timber Ridge, wouldn't you say?"

Before she could answer, Chief Hurley asked, "How should I know?"

"I was talking to Maddy," I said.

"That sounds about right to me," my sister said.

"Are you heading toward town or away from it?"

"Toward," Maddy said.

"I'll be there in nine minutes," he said.

"Are you sure you don't . . . Maddy, did he just hang up on us?"

"He must have, unless there's a dead spot in my coverage here." She leaned forward and closed her phone. I doubted that her action looked that suspicious from the distance Bernie Maine was from us, but something must have spooked him. At the next intersection of an old country road, he pulled off abruptly.

I did a wide U-turn on the shoulder as I told Maddy, "Call the chief and tell him what's going on."

"Yee-haw, I just love a high-speed car chase," she said.

"When you tell him that, try to find a way to word it so that his head doesn't explode," I said as I pulled my car onto the road Maine had just taken. It was paved for fifty feet before it changed into a dirt road, and I could see the dust springing up like a plume behind the BMW.

"Hang on," I said as I pressed the accelerator down closer to the floor.

"Chief, we had to take a detour on Meadowbrook," Maddy said out loud as soon as he answered. I was glad we were on speakerphone again, no matter how the chief of police felt about it.

That was when it hit me. In my haste to follow our suspect, I'd completely missed the name of the road we were on, a crucial bit of information that my sister provided. Then again, I'd been pretty intent on not driving into a tree, so my attention had been focused elsewhere, like on not killing us.

"What are you doing there?" he screamed. "You were supposed to drive straight to Timber Ridge."

"There was a change of plans," I said as I fought my car's desire to become airborne. "Bernie got suspicious and shot down a side road."

"And you had to turn around and follow him. Is that it?"

"What choice did we have? We couldn't just let him get away," I protested.

"Listen to me. You are to stop your car immediately, pull over, and wait for me. Do you both understand?"

"You . . . break . . . can't . . . ," Maddy said in a stuttering voice before she hung up. "What do you think, Eleanor? Was that convincing?" she asked.

"I bought it, and I was sitting right here beside you." When I looked ahead again, I lost sight of Maine's car in some tortuous twist. The road was now more of a path than a legitimate country lane, and I had to wonder if Maine was going to run out of room soon. The real question then would be, what would we do with him if we caught him? I tried not to think about that and focused on the road ahead instead.

It was a good thing that I did, too.

We hit a patch of gravel I spotted barely just in time, and as the front tires hit it, I felt us start to spin. Fighting down my sense of panic, I remembered from a driver's ed class a long time ago to turn into the skid. It didn't save us completely, as we slid off the shoulder and nearly hit a tree, but it kept us both from being injured, and that was a win in my book any day.

"Are you okay?" I asked Maddy as I tried to start the car back up.

"I'm just peachy. Now I know what an ice cube feels like in a blender."

I wanted to continue the chase, but my vehicle had other ideas about that.

The car wouldn't start. Maybe it was flooded. I gave it two minutes and then tried again.

Nothing.

I got out, and Maddy joined me. After I popped the hood open and looked inside the engine compartment, Maddy asked, "Sis, do you have any idea what you're looking at?"

"No. I took home ec, not shop," I said.

"My, how our public educations have let us down," she answered.

A minute later the chief of police drove up and parked with his front bumper nearly touching mine.

"Forget about us. Go after him!" I said a little louder than I should have.

"He's long gone," the chief said. "He must have cut back onto the highway, because if he'd stayed on this dirt path, he would have had to run me off the road to get past me." He glanced at my car and asked nonchalantly, "Having car troubles?"

"It won't start," I admitted.

He reached under the hood, fiddled with something, and then said, "Try it now."

Still nothing, not even a whir, a grind, or a grunt.

"Sorry," the police chief said. "That's the sum total of my car knowledge. Should I call Bob Pickering and have him come out and tow this to his shop?"

I put the hood down on the Subaru, patted it affectionately, and then said, "You might as well. We're not going to be moving otherwise."

"Let me see if I can get him," he said and then looked at Maddy for a second. "Besides, your phones don't get reception out here, do they?"

Maddy pulled out her phone and acted surprised. "Hey, I've got bars now. Imagine that. We must have been in a dead spot."

"If you'd caught up with Bernie Maine, that's exactly what might have happened. I distinctly remember telling the two of you to stay away from him," he said.

"Do you see him anywhere around here?" Maddy asked.

"Maddy, you're not nearly as funny as you think you are."

After the chief talked to Bob and gave him directions to where we were, I said, "I'll stay here with the car. Maddy, maybe the chief here will give you a ride back into town."

"You don't have to," the police chief said. "Bob said that he had his own key to your car. Is your Subaru in the shop that much?"

"Not often, but it runs in spells," I admitted. I glanced at my watch and saw that if we didn't hurry, we were going to be late getting the Slice ready to open for the day. "Is there any chance you could give us a ride to the pizzeria?"

"I don't see why not."

"Can I ride in back?" Maddy asked. "I've always wanted to be a perp. Isn't that what you call them?"

"Maybe they do on television," he said. "I don't care where you sit, if you don't. Eleanor, do you want to ride back there with her?"

"No, thanks," I said. "I'll sit up front with you, if you don't mind."

"Then let's go."

As we drove, Kevin repeated his earlier scolding. "That was incredibly reckless of you to follow him like that."

"Hey, he started it," Maddy said from the back.

"It doesn't matter who started what. I told you that the man was armed. I'm just afraid how it might have ended."

"Do you really think that he's that dangerous?" I asked Chief Hurley. "He's a businessman, for goodness' sake."

"You tell me. One man's dead, and Bernie Maine is one of my prime suspects. How much more dangerous can you get?"

"So, do you really think he did it?" Maddy asked, peeking her head out from the cage that separated us.

"I like him for it better than most of the other suspects on my list," Chief Hurley said.

"Hang on a second," Maddy said. "Did you just share something with us?"

"Sorry. It won't happen again," Chief Hurley said as he shook his head. As much as I loved my sister, there were times when I wanted to stick a sock in her mouth.

"Chief, I still can't figure out why Bernie was following us. It was pretty risky, wasn't it, given that you've been looking for him all day?"

"Is that a jab coming from you, too, Eleanor?"

"No way. I know how slippery the man can be. But why is he so interested in us? We're not making any progress at all."

"Who knows? He's got to realize that the two of you have been digging into his life these past couple of days. Maybe he thinks you got lucky and stumbled across something that could nail him. After all, even a blind pig finds an acorn every now and then."

I wasn't sure I liked the analogy, but I wasn't about to comment on it. "So, does that mean that you've written off Rebecca, Samantha, and Kenny?" I wasn't about to include Bob's and David's names in that particular roster.

He shook his head. "Like I said, Maine's the most likely, but nobody's been eliminated. To be honest, I'm kind of surprised that you left Vivian Wright off of your list."

"That's because Art Young got us her alibi," Maddy said.

I turned and stared hard at my sister, and she got the message immediately. Maddy made a motion as though she was locking up her lips, but if she was, I wanted the key so nothing else could slip out "accidentally."

"How did he manage to do that?" Chief Hurley asked.

"I'm not sure," I said, "but the man I spoke to felt as though Art's involvement was enough to ensure that he was telling the truth."

"I thought you two were through," the chief said.

"We were, but we're back on again."

"So you got him to use a little muscle for you to get what you wanted. Are you sure that this is really a guy you want as a friend?" the chief asked. He made no bones about his displeasure with my renewed friendship.

"He doesn't give me any grief about you being one of my friends, so why should you care about him?"

Chief Hurley took his gaze off the road for a second to look at me. "Are we friends, Eleanor?"

"Well, if you had asked me before, I would have said yes, but hearing that question, now I'm not so sure."

"Easy. I didn't mean anything by it. To be honest, I'm flattered that you feel that way."

"I'll be your friend, too, if I can turn on the siren," Maddy said.

I looked back at her, and she just grinned. Evidently, riding in the back of a squad car was making her feel a little goofy. If that were the case, I was going to make sure that it didn't happen again anytime soon.

The chief ignored her request, and soon enough, we were in front of the Slice. I wasn't sure about the message it was sending to the rest of Timber Ridge for us to climb out of a patrol car, but I couldn't do anything about it.

"Thanks for the ride," I said as I opened the door.

"Hey, there aren't any handles back here," Maddy protested.

The chief smiled at me for a brief second, showing a glimpse once again of the young man I'd been crazy about in high school. "What do you think, Eleanor? Should I drive her around the block once or twice before I let her out?"

I smiled back at him. "You'd better not. She might get to like it and ask you to do it again sometime."

"That's a good point," he said as he unlocked the back door from his control panel.

Maddy climbed out, and as the chief started to drive away, he said, "Be careful, you two."

"You've got it," I said.

After he was gone, I said, "I know it's going to be anticlimactic after that high-speed car chase and taking a ride in the back of a genuine police cruiser, but do you feel like making some pizza?"

"It's almost always my first choice of things to do," Maddy said. "Sorry about all of that blabbing earlier. I don't know what got into me."

"I don't either," I said. "I was about to strangle you at one point."

"Then I'm glad that there was a cage between us," Maddy said with a grin.

I was about to unlock the front door when I saw that someone had written something on the window glass. In the gaudiest shade of red lipstick I'd ever seen, it said BACK OF in bright letters. It was written in block print, and I doubted there was a single fingerprint anywhere near it that belonged to the person who had written it, but I pulled out my phone and called the chief of police, anyway.

"I can't leave you two alone for three minutes, can I?" he asked after he drove back to the Slice and got out of his squad car. Being the chief of police gave him the privilege of driving straight onto the brick-paved promenade, and he'd been known to take advantage of it before. "Where is it?" he asked.

I pointed to the door as Maddy said, "We keep wondering what we're supposed to do with the back of something."

"You both know they meant to say, 'Back off,' " the chief said. "Whoever was writing it was obviously interrupted before they could finish."

"Do you think someone saw them doing this?" I asked as I looked across the promenade for any potential witnesses. Unfortunately, the square was deserted.

"I don't have any idea." Chief Hurley pulled out his camera from the trunk of his car and took a few pictures. After that, he took some powder and dusted it on the glass.

Nothing showed up at all.

"When was the last time you cleaned this?" he asked.

I shrugged, but Maddy said, "Josh cleaned it right before he left last night. He wanted something to do since it was kind of quiet, and I didn't see what it could hurt."

"Probably nothing," the chief said. "I was hoping for a palm or a fingerprint, though." The police chief packed up his little kit and then returned it and the camera to the trunk of his car.

"That's it?" I asked. "That's all you're going to do?"

"I'll have one of my men canvass the area in case someone saw something, but I wouldn't get my hopes up." He could see that I wasn't happy with the minimal effort, so he asked me, "Eleanor, what else do you want me to do?"

"Nothing," I said. "You're right. I just hate that someone tried to scare us off like that."

"As threats go, it's a pretty benign one," Chief Hurley said. "Here's some cleaner and a few paper towels you can use to get rid of it. This is pretty powerful stuff, so go wash your hands as soon as you are finished with it."

"Hang on a second," Maddy said as she pulled out her cell phone and took a few pictures herself. "Go on. I got it," she answered.

After I cleaned the window and handed the spray bottle back to the chief, he said, "If there's nothing else, I'm going to take off."

"See you later," I answered. "Thanks for coming back so quickly."

"That's my job, to serve and protect. Seriously, though, call me if *anything* comes up, no matter how trivial it might seem to be to you."

"We'll do our best," I said.

He let that slide as he got into his cruiser and drove away.

"Still feel like making pizza?" I asked Maddy.

"Now more than ever. A little normalcy would be nice right about now."

Unfortunately, that ended up being the last thing we got.

Chapter 16

"Eleanor, Maddy says she needs you up front," Greg said as he came into the kitchen a little later. He was working double shifts to make up for his absence lately, and we were glad to have him. "She said to tell you that it's important."

"Tell her I'll be right there," I said as I slipped the final pizza order onto the conveyor. Peeking in through the other side of the oven, I saw that I had around five minutes before the first sandwich on the conveyor was due to come out.

I walked out to the dining room, wondering what was so urgent, and that was when I saw my sister talking to Rebecca Whitmore.

As I approached them, Maddy said, "Okay, she's

here now. Now go ahead. What was it that you wanted to tell me?"

"I found some money in the hidden drawer, just like you said, and I thought that it was only fair to split it with you," she said as she started digging around in her purse.

"That's really nice of you," Maddy said, "but if it's a lot of money, you don't have to give me half." We both knew that ten thousand was substantial, and it was odd that Rebecca was being so generous.

When she pulled out a slim envelope, there was more than cash there, though. "All I need is for you to sign a waiver for the rest of Mom's stuff, and half the money is yours."

"So, you're trying to buy me off, is that it?" Maddy asked, not taking the envelope.

"Believe me, I'm doing you a favor. All that Mom left behind were bills and two mortgages. There's not going to be anything left, so I'd advise you to take this and be happy that you're done with it."

"Well, I can't sign anything until I know how much we're talking about," Maddy replied, studying the skinny envelope. Unless Rebecca had deposited the money and written her a check, there was no way that there was five grand in there.

"I'd really rather it was a surprise," Rebecca said stubbornly. "Does it honestly matter how much it is? This is pure profit for you." She pulled out another copy of the waiver we'd seen before and handed it to Maddy, along with a pen.

My sister promptly put them both down on a nearby table without signing anything. "Sorry, but I don't think I'll be able to sign anything without knowing what you're offering me in return."

Rebecca started to pout a little and then shrugged. "Fine. Spoil the surprise." She opened the envelope again and pulled out five one-hundred-dollar bills. "Think about what you could do with that money."

"This is half of what you found?" Maddy said as she looked at the anemic pile of cash.

"Right down the middle," Rebecca said, averting her gaze for a moment as she said it.

Maddy shook her head. "Thanks, but no thanks. I wouldn't take it if it were ten times that much." I echoed her smile, since we both knew that the real amount from an equal split would be exactly that, five thousand dollars.

Rebecca glanced at me quickly, and I did my best to kill my smile.

"You're making a huge mistake," she said to Maddy.

My sister picked up the waiver and the pen and handed them back to Rebecca. "Maybe so. It wouldn't be the first time, and I'm pretty sure that it won't be the last. Have you decided what you're going to do with the house?"

"I'm moving in, at least for now. I managed to scrape up eight grand to pay off most of the bills, including the second mortgage, so I'll be okay for a while."

What a coincidence. After taking eight of the ten grand from the drawer to pay off the second, she *still* wasn't giving Maddy half of what was left. I wouldn't trust the woman to count my fingers for me.

"Funny, I wouldn't think you'd choose to live there after what happened to your brother and mother," Maddy said.

"Mom died at the hospital, and Grant was murdered over there across the square," she said as she pointed to the spot on the promenade. "Besides, it's going to take a long time to go through everything at the house, and it will be quite a bit easier if I'm staying there to do it. I wouldn't want to miss anything. It was important to my mother, you understand."

Maddy shrugged. "Whatever you say. Let me know when you're ready to file for probate. I have a vested interest, you know, and I want to be there."

"Of course," Rebecca said through gritted teeth. Maddy was playing with fire. If Grant's sister was indeed the murderer, my sister was adding her name to the list of those most likely to be killed next.

As Rebecca started to leave, Maddy called out, "And don't forget to include the thousand dollars you found in your assessment."

"What thousand are you talking about?" Rebecca asked curiously.

"Well, that's how much you found in the drawer. That's right, isn't it? Half of a thousand is five hundred, and that's what you just offered me."

"Certainly," Rebecca said, and then she was gone.

"My, that was fun," Maddy said.

"Would you come into the kitchen with me? The next sandwich should be ready to serve now."

She followed me in, and the second the kitchen door was closed, I asked her, "Did you enjoy yourself just now?"

"I've been wanting to tweak her since the day we met quite a few years ago. Yes, I'd have to say that as amusements go, that was right up there."

"Maddy, we both know that she was lying about the money she found, but what good did it do to let her know that we were aware of the fact that she was cheating you?"

Maddy frowned. "Okay, maybe it wasn't the smartest thing that I could have done, but I couldn't let her think that she had outsmarted me. You know why she's staying at the house, don't you? Sentiment has nothing to do with it."

"Obviously, she wants to find every last dollar Grant hid," I said. "And that's going to take some time. She probably will, too. A hundred and fifty thousand dollars can't be that easy to hide, don't you think?"

"If Grant had an entire house to do it in, it just might be, but she's got time on her side, and if it's stashed there, she's bound to find it eventually."

"Not if we find it first," I said.

"How can we do that? We don't even have access to the place anymore."

"I don't know, but I hate the thought of her getting away with it."

"Murder or theft?" Maddy asked me.

"Well, we *know* she's a thief. We just need to figure out if she's a killer or not."

I took the sandwich out, slid it onto a tray, and then cut it in half.

"When you know how we can do that, be sure to let me know," Maddy said as she picked the sandwich up and left to deliver it.

Josh came into the kitchen ten minutes before we were set to close for our own lunch break. Maddy and I had been discussing all afternoon what we were going to do to investigate, but so far we hadn't come up with anything concrete.

"You aren't due to start your shift until we get back from lunch," I said. "Greg's working a double shift, so we don't need you until then."

"I'm not here to work," Josh said. "I was digging around on the Internet, and I found something I thought you'd like to see."

"What is it?" I asked.

He handed me a printout from his computer, and I saw that it was an announcement. Samantha and Kenny Stout were playing an afternoon show in Grayson's Corners, not too far away from Timber Ridge.

I read it and then handed the printout back to him. "Surely they canceled it. Samantha can't even stand to be in the same town as her ex-husband, let alone share a stage with him."

"I just called, and they started playing ten minutes ago."

"Both of them?" I asked, having a hard time believing that Samantha would play with Kenny after what she'd told Maddy and me earlier.

"Both of them," he said. "If you close the Slice now, you can get there before the fireworks start."

"Why would anyone have fireworks in the middle of the afternoon?"

"I didn't mean literally," he said, "but just because they started their show doesn't mean they'll necessarily finish it."

There was nothing in the oven, so it was an easy decision to make. "Come with me," I said as I flipped off the conveyor.

There were two single diners in the Slice, so I walked to the door and flipped the sign that told our customers that we were closed. After locking the door, I told our remaining diners, "Take your time. I'm not trying to rush you. You still have ten minutes."

Maddy and Greg walked over to us. "What's going on?"

"We're going to Grayson's Corners right now," I

explained, "and the boys are going to clean up for us as soon as our patrons leave. Right, guys?"

"We'd rather go with you," Josh said. "What if there's trouble?"

"If there is, we can handle it," I said. "What do you say? Will you do this for us?"

"Of course we will," Greg said.

"Why exactly are we going to Grayson's Corners?" Maddy asked as she took off her apron. "Are we eating lunch at Mama Mia's?"

"Not today. Samantha and Kenny are playing on an outdoor stage there right now, and if we hurry, we might just get a chance to grill them a little more before they're both gone for good."

"What are we waiting for, then? Let's go," she said.

I unlocked the door, and Greg closed it behind us.

As we walked through the shortcut, Maddy said with a grin, "I've got an idea. Why don't I drive?"

"You are so funny," I said deadpan.

"Have you heard from Bob Pickering yet?"

"He says that a wire came loose somewhere," I said, "and that I was probably driving too fast on a bad road."

"That sounds like a really technical diagnosis. It's a good thing he's such a veteran mechanic," Maddy said. "Why hasn't he brought it back over here yet?"

"He found a few other things wrong when he

was poking around under the hood," I admitted. "I should have it by this evening."

"I'm glad you can trust Bob. Otherwise, it would sound like too big a coincidence that he found other problems while he was under the hood, you know?"

"Sure, but he'll do right by me. He always has."

"Let's go," Maddy said as she unlocked her car. "Just a warning, but I might speed a little."

"Be my guest, but you're paying for the ticket if you get one."

"Me? Didn't you know, Eleanor? I'm too charming to get a speeding ticket."

"Just keep telling yourself that, and maybe someday it will be true."

When we got to the outdoor stage, though, it appeared that we were too late. No one was playing, and the people who had gathered for the show were milling about as though they were waiting for something that might not happen. The band's logo from the notice I'd seen, STOUTER THAN MOST, was on the stage, but neither performer was there. In the crowd I spotted Jenny Wilkes, the woman who ran the flower shop in town, but she didn't see me. It was just as well. I didn't really have time to stop and chat.

"We missed it," Maddy said, dejected that another lead had dead-ended on us.

THE MISSING DOUGH

I was about to agree when I saw a flash of something backstage. "Follow me," I said softly and tugged lightly on Maddy's arm.

As we neared the back area, I could hear a loud conversation going on. Argument was probably more like it. Kenny was clearly angry about something, and Samantha was doing her best to hold up her end under the attack from her ex-husband.

"I'm not going to do it, and I don't care what you think," I heard Samantha say.

"If you don't now, then you'd better start," Kenny said as he moved closer to her. "Neither one of us can afford to have those two nosy sisters keep digging into our business. You've got to stop going to them every time we have a little spat."

"That wasn't a little spat," she countered.

"Do you want to know something? That's your problem, Samantha. You blow everything out of proportion and read things into the simplest actions. You've got to stop and think about what you're saying before you open your mouth," he said with an ominous pause.

"It sounds like there's an 'or else' somewhere in there," Samantha said.

"There you go again. I know how important it is to you that you're the bride at every wedding and the corpse at every funeral, but the world doesn't spin that way."

"I'm not like that," she said defiantly.

"Try telling that to someone who was never married to you. The more I think about it, the more I realize that was probably the biggest mistake I ever made in my life."

"Me too," she said so softly that I could barely hear her.

"What was that?"

Instead of answering, Samantha pointed to her watch. "Our break is over. We just have to go on for fifteen more minutes, and then we're finished. This is my last show with you, Kenny. After today I never want to see you again."

"You don't really mean that, do you?" he said, his voice getting low and mean. "How are you going to avoid it? We both know that I am going to be in this area forever, and so are you."

"I can do whatever I want to. You don't own me. The days of you telling me what to do are long gone."

"Do you honestly believe that's true?" he asked, and I saw Samantha step back just a little. When she didn't answer his question, he added, "Remember, no more talking to anyone about anything that concerns me. I have some errands to run after the show, but we'll discuss this later, I promise you."

"Whatever," she said shakily.

"Do us both a favor and try not to cause me any more trouble in the meantime, okay?"

As they headed for the stage, I pulled Maddy back behind a bush so they wouldn't see us. They walked past us and mounted the platform to the cheers from the crowd. As they started to play, Samantha's voice was a little shaky at first, but she quickly got it back.

"And I thought *I* had some bad ex-husbands," Maddy said. "He's really not a nice man, is he?"

"Kenny's not my favorite guy in the world, there's no doubt about that," I agreed. "Why do you suppose he was so upset that she'd been talking to us?"

"Think about it. Would you want someone sharing their opinions of you if you were *that* guy? I know I wouldn't."

"No, there's got to be more to it than that. It was almost as though he was afraid she'd tell us something that would incriminate him, you know?"

"It's possible. If we're lucky, we'll find out, anyway."

"Hey, ladies, did we miss anything?" Josh asked from right behind me, nearly scaring me out of my shoes.

"What are you doing here?" I asked.

"Greg's with me, too. He's finding a parking space, but he'll be here in a second."

"You didn't answer my question," I said.

"We were worried about you," he admitted. "Hey, don't be mad."

I couldn't really be after he admitted that. "Thanks, but I'm afraid the two of you wasted a trip."

"We don't mind," he said as Greg rushed up to join us.

"What did we miss?" Greg asked, nearly out of breath.

"They were just fighting backstage," Maddy said.

Greg listened to the music for a second. "You'd never know it right now."

It was true. As I listened to them play, it was clear that they'd found their way again, and it was impossible to tell that there was an ocean of tension between them.

"What do we do? Just hang around and wait for them to finish?" Maddy asked. "I've got a hunch that after what we just heard, neither one of them is going to be in any mood to talk to us."

"We can go back if you want, but it's just going to be another ten minutes," I said. "What could it hurt to try?"

"Let's wait and see what happens," she said.

"Hey, I've seen that before," Greg said as he pointed to the band's logo onstage. "I parked behind an old station wagon with a decal of that on the rear window. You don't think that was Kenny's car, do you?"

"Why do you ask?"

"He must be doing some gardening. When I peeked in through the back window, I saw a pick and shovel in there."

"What makes you think he was gardening? Was there anything else in there, like potting soil or lime?" I asked.

"No, just the tools. Why? Do you think it means anything?" Greg asked.

"Whatever it is, I doubt that it's good news for Samantha. I hate to leave her alone after the show," Maddy said.

"Do you think he's going to kill her and then bury the body somewhere?" Josh asked. He had an overactive imagination as a rule, but this time, my thoughts had followed an identical path to his. "We've got to do something to stop him before it's too late."

"What can we do?" Maddy asked. "We have a pizzeria to run."

I had a sudden inspiration. "Josh, how would you and Greg like to do a little detective work? You'll still get paid, but you'd be helping us out a great deal."

"Name it," Greg said, and Josh nodded. It wasn't often that they were able to participate in one of our investigations, especially Josh, but I was going to have to take whatever grief there was about it that Kevin Hurley might dish out later. I needed them right now.

"As soon as they split up, I want Greg to follow Kenny in his car, and, Josh, you can take Maddy's car and follow Samantha. Don't be obvious about it, but don't lose them, either. Can you do that?"

"Sure we can, but there's just one problem," Greg said. "How are you two getting back to Timber Ridge?"

"I spotted Jenny Wilkes in the crowd, so we'll catch a ride back with her."

"What if she's not going straight back to Timber Ridge?" Maddy asked.

"Then we'll find some other way home. We're a pair of resourceful women. We'll manage somehow, even if we have to call David or Bob to come pick us up."

From the stage, I heard Samantha say, "Thanks for coming, and have a nice day. We're out."

"Hurry," I said. "Maddy, do you mind if Josh drives your car?"

"Why should I?" she asked as she handed him her keys. "After all, he's a certified driving instructor now, right?"

"Right," Josh said, completely missing the sarcasm in her voice.

"What should we do if there's trouble?" Greg asked.

"Call the police chief, and don't interfere unless it's bad, and I mean really bad. Do you both promise to do your best to stay out of trouble?"

They nodded and then split up. Greg went back to his car, while Josh hung around, waiting for Samantha. As we walked past him to where the audience was just breaking up, Maddy pointed and said, "I'm parked over there."

"I already spotted it on the way in," Josh said with a grin.

We couldn't find Jenny at first, and I wasn't thrilled about the prospect of calling David or Bob to come get us, but then Maddy spotted her approaching her floral delivery van.

"Jenny, wait up," we both called out to her as we saw her getting out her keys.

She stopped and then turned and grinned at us. "I didn't know you two were Stout fans. They're pretty wonderful, aren't they?"

"This is the second time we've seen them play this week," I said. "Is there any chance we could catch a ride back to Timber Ridge with you?"

"Where's your car?" she asked.

"It's in the shop even as we speak," I said.

"Sure, hop in. There's just one problem, though," she said.

"Do we have some deliveries to make?" I asked.

"No, the truck's empty, but there's just one extra seat. One of you is going to have to sit on the floor in back."

Maddy laughed. "I'll do it. It'll be just like a hayride on the back of a tractor flatbed."

Jenny grinned. "As a matter of fact, it will be nothing like that, but I guess if you're desperate, it's going to have to do, isn't it? At least the van smells good. I've been driving around with flowers in it for so long, it's like the scents have seeped into the metal, you know?"

"No, but I have a feeling that we're about to find out," I said.

As Jenny opened the back door, I asked Maddy, "Are you sure you don't mind riding in the back?"

"Are you kidding? It sounds like a hoot. Besides, my younger bones will be able to stand up to it better than your brittle old ones."

"I'd argue with you about it, but I might end up losing my nice comfortable seat."

As we drove back to Timber Ridge, Jenny asked, "Have you had any luck finding the killer yet? That's what you two were really doing at the concert, isn't it?"

"You don't miss much that goes on around town, do you?" I asked her.

"Do you mean for a flower lady?"

"I mean for anybody," I said.

"I get around a lot, I talk to a lot of people, and I'm always listening. Momma always said that you don't learn a thing by talking, and she was right."

Jenny's mother had run the flower shop before her, and I knew that the two of them had been close. "You still miss her, don't you?"

"Every day. I imagine it's the same with Joe, even if you do have a new man in your life these days."

I laughed. "Like I said, you don't miss much. Sure, I miss Joe, but it's not so much a hole anymore as it is a sweet feeling of what I was lucky enough to have once."

"And maybe again," she said with a smile.

"You're a hopeless romantic, aren't you?"

"I don't see how I could be a florist unless I was," she admitted.

"How's *your* love life going?" I asked.

"You know me. I'm the one who is always giving the flowers to other people. The last time I actually got them was in high school. It was the first dozen roses I ever got for my very own."

"Was he the love of your life?" I asked. Jenny rarely talked about herself, and I was interested in what had made her such a romantic.

"You'd think so, but no. He was just a sweet guy, naive in the best way, you know? I was sad about another guy breaking up with me, and the two of us were good friends, so he bought me roses to cheer me up. And you know what? It worked."

"Did he ask you out after that? Did you fall in love?" I asked, hoping for a happy ending to the story.

"No, like I said, it wasn't like that. His girlfriend went to a rival school, and they were a great match. Tim just had that kind of heart, you know? I have to admit, though, sometimes I wonder what ever happened to him," she said wistfully, and I wondered if Jenny had wished they were more than just friends after all.

"You should look him up. With the Internet these days, it would have to be pretty easy to find him."

"I've thought about it a few times, but you know what? I think maybe the memory is better than what the reality might be these days."

The more I thought about it, the more I realized that she was probably right. The memory she had from the past was probably too lovely to risk.

Chapter 17

After we parked in front of the flower shop, I went around back and opened the door for Maddy. "How was your ride?" I asked her.

"Adventurous," she answered, clearly a little weary from the trip. "Next time, you get to ride in back."

Since there wasn't much danger of that ever happening, I was quick to agree. "It's a deal."

Jenny joined us, and I hugged her as we stood on the sidewalk in front of her shop. "Thanks again for the ride."

"Honestly, it was fun having the company," she said. "If you want to go with me to the next concert, I'd love to have you."

I knew in my heart that this particular group

would never perform together again, but I didn't have the heart to tell her that. "Sounds great," I said.

As Maddy and I walked to the pizzeria, I asked, "Was it really that bad?"

"No. Once I got the hang of it, it wasn't too tough at all. Did you two have a nice comfy ride up front?"

"It was fine," I said. I wasn't about to tell her how special it had really been. "Now, let's open the pizzeria back up. I'll make 'em in back, and you serve 'em out front. How does that sound?"

"Like it's where we belong," she said with a laugh.

We didn't hear a word from Greg or Josh for quite some time, and I kept checking my cell phone to make sure that it was working. Fortunately, we were pretty busy, but every now and then Maddy would come back and ask, "Have you heard anything yet?"

I'd just shake my head and try not to worry about the possible danger I'd put them both in. It was amazing how responsible I felt for the two grown men. If anything happened to either one of them, I'd never be able to forgive myself.

"Should we call them?" Maddy asked the last time she came in.

"We have to show them that we trust them," I said. "Let's give them a little more time."

I was about to break down and call them anyway when Josh finally showed up first. Maddy followed close on his heels all the way back to the kitchen.

"I couldn't wait to find out what he had to say, and he wouldn't tell me a thing unless you could hear it, too," she explained.

"You've got three minutes until this sandwich is ready to deliver," I said.

She looked at Josh and said, "Then you'd better talk fast."

He shrugged. "Okay, but it's not all that much. After they split up, I followed Samantha, just like you asked me to do."

"Where did she go first?" I asked.

"She headed straight for an Internet café in town. Samantha spent about a half an hour there, and then she went back to her apartment in Cow Spots and didn't budge an inch."

"But that was over two hours ago," I said. "What did you do after that? Were you just waiting outside of her apartment the whole time?"

"Actually, I went back to Grayson's Corners."

"Why did you do that?" Maddy asked.

"I wanted to check the browser history on the computer she was on," Josh admitted.

"You can do that after she's signed off? Didn't she clear it when she left?" I asked.

"She could have, but most folks probably wouldn't be able to find it. Then again, I'm not most people." He pulled a few pages of a computer printout out of his back pocket and handed them to me as he added, "Nobody else had been on the computer she was using, so I was able to call this up."

I read the pages, with Maddy looking over my shoulder. "It's a one-way ticket to London," I said.

"Look when she's leaving." Josh said.

"She's going tomorrow?" I asked. "How can she leave so soon?"

"She was willing to pay a premium price for the ticket," Josh said. "I've got a feeling that she's not coming back anytime soon."

I glanced over at the oven and saw that the sandwich was ready. As I cut it and put it in on a plate, I said, "Maddy, you need to serve this while it's hot."

"Don't say anything until I get back," she said.

"There's nothing else to tell," Josh said. "The second I found this, I came straight here." He handed Maddy her keys. "Thanks for letting me borrow your car."

"I was happy to," she said and then took the food.

After she had left, Josh asked, "Does that mean I'm finished for the night?"

I laughed as I threw his apron at him. "Sorry, but we need you here now. Go ahead and give Maddy a hand out front, okay?"

"You bet," he said.

Before he left, I said, "You did a nice job, Josh."

"Thanks."

There was something I needed to know, but I wasn't sure if I should ask him. Finally, I decided that the suspense of not knowing would be the hardest of all. "Are you going to tell your dad about this?"

"Should I?" he asked as he tied the back of his apron.

I thought about it and began to wonder what the right thing to do was in this situation. A part of me wanted to keep this a secret between us, but how would Kevin feel when he found out that his son might have been withholding valuable information from him when he still had the chance to do something about it? "Call him and tell him what you know," I said.

"Aren't you going to take some heat because of it?"

"Don't worry about me. He needs to hear about what's going on before it's too late to do anything about it," I said.

"If you're sure that's what you want me to do," Josh said as he pulled out his phone.

"You'd better call him right now before I change my mind."

Josh made the call, and after a minute of conversation, he handed me the phone. "He wants to talk to you."

I wasn't thrilled to take the phone, but I didn't have much choice. "Chief, I didn't mean to get your son involved, but I thought that it was important."

"We'll talk about that later," he said. "For now, I just wanted to let you know that we're pretty sure we know who killed Grant, and it wasn't Samantha Stout."

"So, you're fine if she leaves the country? Are you that sure?"

"Why? Is there something you're not telling me?" he asked.

"You know what I know. Hey, I should get a little credit for having Josh call you with new information, even though I knew you were going to chew me out because of it."

"Okay, I'll take it easy on you. Listen, I've got to go. Try not to get him involved in any more murder cases, no matter how wrong you might be about who you suspect, okay? I've got only one kid, and I'd kind of like to keep him around."

"Understood," I said, and then he hung up on me.

"That went better than I thought it would," Josh said as he took his phone back from me.

"Why do you say that?"

"I didn't hear him yell at you even once," he answered with the whisper of a grin.

"Well, he wasn't happy with me," I said, "but I think we're okay."

"He probably thinks he's already got the bad guy in his sights. Did I do all of that for nothing?"

"Josh, we never know what's going to be useful and what's not. I stand by what I said before. You did good. Now, get to work," I said with a smile.

"Yes, Ma'am," he replied.

After he left, I started cleaning up a little, since I was still waiting for two pizzas to make it through the conveyor oven. Was Chief Hurley right? Could Samantha be a dead end? And who did he believe was the killer? Was it Maine, an obvious choice, or maybe even Kenny? I wasn't ready to name the killer myself, no matter how confident the police chief had sounded on the telephone.

Greg came in less than half an hour later. Maddy walked in with him, and I asked, "Where's Josh? I thought he'd want to hear this, too."

"He's manning the front," she said.

"And he agreed to that?" I asked, knowing his high level of curiosity.

"Well, let's just say that I pulled rank on him and leave it at that, okay?"

"Okay," I said as I turned to Greg. "Did you have any luck?"

"I wasn't sure at first, but it ended up with a bang. It was a good idea to follow him, Eleanor."

"He didn't go back to Samantha's place, did he?" I had a sudden sense of dread that Josh had left her alone at exactly the wrong time. She wouldn't be safe until she was on that plane.

"No, but that doesn't mean he won't," Greg said.

"Tell us what happened," I said.

"Well, at first he went to the garden center and bought some flowers, some fertilizer, and some bagged mulch. It looked as though he was going to use that shovel and pick for exactly what most folks would, and I was about to give up, but you said to follow him, so I did. The next place he stopped was at Parker's Furniture, and I thought I was really wasting my time. At least I did until he came out."

"Why? What was he doing?"

"He had a huge footlocker with him," Greg said. "It took him twenty minutes to tie it to the roof of his car, and at one point I was about to help him secure it myself just to get things moving along again."

"You didn't, though, did you?" I asked.

"No, as tempting as it was, I sat in the car and waited. After he got it latched down securely, he drove to his place in Cow Spots, but he didn't unload the footlocker. In fact, everything stayed right there in his station wagon."

"Why is that significant?" Maddy asked.

"He's renting a place on the outskirts of town," Greg said. "The yard's not much bigger than a postage stamp, but there are enough woods behind his place to get lost in."

"What do you think he's going to do?"

"I don't know," Greg admitted, "but I don't like it. Maybe my imagination's just getting the best of me, but that footlocker was big enough to bury a body in."

"You think he's going to kill Samantha before she gets a chance to escape?" I asked.

"That was the first thing I thought of. There's something else, too. When he was inside the furniture store shopping, I casually walked past his station wagon so I could take a closer look at those tools."

"You shouldn't have taken that kind of chance," I said.

"He doesn't even know me, though. We never met, remember?"

"So, what did you see?" Maddy asked.

"The tools had been used recently. There was still red clay sticking to both of them. I've got a feeling that he's already dug his hole."

I felt a chill run through me as he said it. "You really think he's going to kill her, don't you?"

"It's a distinct possibility," Greg said. "Should we call the police chief?"

"He might already know about it," I said. "He hinted earlier that he was close to catching someone."

"What if he's after somebody else, though?" Greg asked. "If something happens to Samantha and there was anything I could do to stop it, I don't know if I'd ever be able to forgive myself."

"Hang on," I said as the kitchen door opened and Bob Lemon walked in.

He was smiling broadly, as though the weight of the world had been lifted off his shoulders. "Ladies, I've got good news."

"That's great to hear, because we could sure use some," Maddy said after she kissed him.

"The police chief has invited me to join him when he arrests Grant's killer," he said proudly.

"You're off the hook?" Maddy asked, hugging him tightly.

"Yes, I've been officially cleared of the crime," he said.

I didn't care who solved the murder, just as long as someone did. "Then who killed Grant? Was it Kenny Stout?"

"No, the chief is convinced that it was Bernie Maine. He found Grant's wallet when he searched Maine's place a second time, and an envelope with fifteen hundred dollars in it was right beside it. The wallet had a spatter of blood on it, too, and it looks like Maine took it off the body after he skewered Grant."

"It's still just circumstantial, though, isn't it?" I asked.

"You're not upset just because you didn't figure it out first, are you? The police chief has advantages and resources that you don't. You shouldn't be so hard on yourself."

"That's not it at all," I said. "How is he going to catch Bernie, even if he believes that he's the killer? The man has just vanished since Maddy and I chased him down that country road."

"The chief had an idea, and he was going through some papers of Maine's and found a Web site address for a realty company in Grayson's Corners. It seems that old Bernie rented a remote cabin in the woods two weeks ago, and the chief is pretty sure he's holing up there."

"Can we come, too?" Maddy asked.

"Sorry. He let me tell you, but I'm the only civilian that's going to be included. I'll give you a call when it's all over, though, I promise," he told Maddy and then gave her another kiss. "Thank you all for all of your hard work. I'm sure Chief Hurley couldn't have done it without you."

Once he was gone, Maddy said, "Well, I guess we were wrong, Sis."

"I'm not so sure," I said.

Greg said, "Even if someone else is the killer, I'm still worried about Samantha. Kenny Stout may not have killed Grant, but that doesn't mean that he's not capable of murdering his ex-wife. Eleanor, I'd like to go over there and make sure nothing's happened to her, and I know that Josh is going to want to go, too. Is there any way we can get off early?"

I looked at the clock and saw that we had an hour left on our evening shift, but Greg was right. If we could stop something bad from happening, then we should. "Go on. We'll handle this. But don't do anything crazy, okay?"

"We won't," Greg said, and then he took off.

"It looks like it's just the two of us again," I said to Maddy as we walked out of the kitchen. The dining room was almost empty, with one couple waiting for their pizza.

"I know. It feels as though we're missing out on all of the action."

"I've got an idea." I approached the couple and said, "I've got a deal for you tonight, one night only. If you get your pizza as a carryout, it's free, and so are two sodas of your choice. How does that sound?"

"Like a winner," the man said. His companion started to protest, so he added, "I'll watch *Morning Glory* with you again if we can eat in front of the TV."

"But you hate chick flicks," she said, softening slightly.

"Maybe so, but I love you," he said.

"It's a deal, then," she said as she turned to me.

I pulled out the pizza, boxed it, cut it, and then carried it back out. Maddy had already given them their drinks.

"I feel like we're taking advantage of you," the man said.

"Honestly, you're doing us a favor," I said as I let them out and locked the door behind them.

"That was brilliant," Maddy said. "Only now what do we do?"

"Something's been nagging me ever since we first went over those papers we took from Grant's apartment. Would you mind indulging me so we can go home and look at them again?"

"If you have a hunch, we should go with it," she said.

It felt odd closing up the pizza place early, but there was a special mood in the air tonight, as though something big was about to happen, and I didn't want to miss out on it.

* * *

We got back to my place, and before we could even take our jackets off, I headed for the bench where Maddy and I had stored the papers we'd found. It just took a second for me to find what I was looking for.

On the back of one of the pages in front of us was the piece of paper covered with a scribble of numbers that were all crossed out with single lines. I'd noticed it before, but I'd been distracted before I'd had a chance to examine it closely. Something Bob had said about a Web site address had stuck in my mind, because it was out of place.

When I looked at the paper again, there it was.

Among the clutter of useless information, I found what had to be a Web site address.

"Maddy, pop out your magic telephone for me, would you?"

"I'd be glad to. Who are we calling?" she asked as she dug her phone out of her purse.

"Nobody. I want to see what this site is all about."

I handed her the piece of paper, pointed out the Web address, and she nodded as she typed a few keys on her phone pad. After a few seconds, she pulled up the site and then said, "I wonder what this means."

"What did you find?" I asked.

She showed me her phone, and I saw an image on the screen, something that looked like an aerial view of someone's house and yard.

"Whose place is this?" I asked as I searched for clues in what we could see.

"Hang on a second and I can tell you." She went through a few steps, and after more than three hundred of the promised seconds had passed, she finally said, "I'll be. It's Sharon Whitmore's place."

"I don't get it," I said. "Why would Grant care about the view of the house where he was living? If anyone would know what it was like there, it would be him."

She returned to the first screen and then tapped a few buttons on her phone, blowing up the view. "Eleanor, what does that look like to you?"

I stared at the small screen for a moment, and then I finally realized what I was seeing. "It's a freshly dug hole, if I had to guess. What does it mean, though?"

"Come on. Grab your coat. I want to see what Grant Whitmore buried in the yard."

"How long ago was this shot taken?" I asked. "What makes you think there's even anything there now?"

"Look at the date. It was taken sometime last week, so there's bound to still be signs that he'd been digging."

"How did he even know that this photograph was there?" I asked.

"He could have checked the website occasionally. I know other folks that do that. It must have given him a heart attack when he saw the image on the screen."

"Maddy, what are we going to do? Go over there with shovels and try to unearth who knows what after midnight? Besides, he probably moved whatever he buried there the second he saw fresh dirt."

"Maybe not. There's a chance that he didn't have enough time to do anything about it before he was murdered."

"So, we're going to go find out for ourselves."

"What other choice do we have?" Maddy asked me. "If we wait until tomorrow, we might be too late."

"Okay. Let's do this before my sanity starts creeping in," I said. "I have a shovel and a pick in the basement, but my flashlight batteries are just about dead."

Chapter 18

"I don't think we'll need the batteries, anyway," Maddy said as she pointed outside. "There's a full moon out tonight."

"That's just going to make it easier for someone to spot us. We should have some kind of cover story to explain what we're doing before we go."

She just smiled and shook her head. "If you can think of *anything* that would make any sense to anyone who might catch us, then you're three steps ahead of me."

"Okay, then it will be on to Plan B," I said as we changed into the darkest clothes we had.

"What's Plan B?" Maddy asked.

"If someone comes by while we're digging, we drop the tools and run."

"That sounds good to me."

"Hey, who said we couldn't plan things out?" I asked. "But instead of dropping our tools when we take off running, we have to take them with us. They belonged to Joe before we got married, and I'll be hanged if I just leave them behind."

"That's what I love about you, Eleanor. You're practical to the end. We might not know who killed Grant, but at least we have a shot at retrieving the money he probably buried there. It's not perfect, but it's better than nothing."

We parked down the street after driving past Sharon's house. I was afraid that Rebecca might still be awake, but there were no signs of her, so hopefully she'd be sound asleep, like any sane person would be at that hour of the night. Maddy and I walked together in the darkness, ready to run the moment we saw anyone's headlights, but thankfully we didn't see anyone as we made our way into the yard.

"Where was that spot exactly?" Maddy asked, peering around in the darkness. Though there was light from the moon, it was obscured by clouds that had come barreling in, and we were left with flashes of illumination, only to be plunged into darkness and, just as quickly, back out again. In addition, the view from ground level was quite a bit different from the one looking straight down from a satellite. It took me a moment to orient myself, and then I spotted the largest tree we'd seen in the image.

"It's got to be right over there," I said as I led the way.

"There it is," Maddy hissed when she spotted the disturbed soil, and we both hurried toward it.

"Let's start digging," I said.

As we worked at removing the clay soil, Maddy asked, "Do you think there's a chance that Bernie Maine really killed Grant?"

"I don't think so, but the chief of police does," I said. The repacked hole was tougher to dig than I thought it would be, and we were having a difficult time breaking up the soil even using the pick. "Maine seems like he's the type who would get his money back before he killed Grant. He's still hanging around here, though, and he's following us, so I think that means that he doesn't have the money himself."

"What about the others?" Maddy asked as she took the pick from me and drove it home. The clay began to break up a little easier once we got past the top crust of it, and my shovel went in easier this time. It actually felt as though we were making some real progress. "Wouldn't any reasonable person want to have that money before they killed the only person who knew where the cash was?"

I nodded as I pulled another shovelful out. "Nobody's run yet, so whoever killed Grant is obviously still looking for the money." I stuck the shovel back in the hole and wiped my brow. This was harder going than I'd ever imagined. "That could mean that the murder was an act of passion instead of greed."

"Well, all three of our remaining suspects could have had *that* motivation," Maddy said. "Kenny was jealous of Grant, Rebecca felt that her brother was cheating her, and Samantha had *both* motivations."

I started to dig again, but then I stopped. "What's the difference between the three of them, then? We know that Rebecca and Kenny plan to hang around, and Samantha is the only one leaving, isn't she? Doesn't that look bad on her?"

"She's fleeing an abusive ex," Maddy said. "That's reason enough for her to escape, isn't it?"

"Only if we believe her. Think about it, Maddy. Every time we've heard her interact with Kenny, she's played the victim, but what if she was just doing it to divert suspicion away from herself? She clearly knows which buttons of Kenny's to push, so it wouldn't be all that hard to get him to lose his temper whenever they were together. It would make a pretty convincing argument for her to run away."

"What about the money, though? Doesn't she care about that?"

I dug another scoop of soil out. "How about this? What if she believes that it's already lost to her? She waited around long enough so that it wouldn't look suspicious when she finally left, and Kenny gave her the perfect excuse. You know, Chief Hurley was right. We have no outside verification that *anything* she told us about him abusing her is true."

"But we heard them together," Maddy protested. "He was clearly threatening her."

"At the pizzeria she could have been playing us," I said. "What if she already had her exit planned and was just setting us up as her alibis for running?"

"Maybe that's true, but what about what we overheard backstage? Eleanor, there's no way that she even knew that we were there."

"I'm not sure that she didn't see us, but even so, she was egging him on. Sure, he was bossy and pushier with her than either one of us would ever stand for, but did he say anything that would make us think that he was capable of murder? Remember when he had the stun gun and refused to use it on us?"

"The way you tell it is pretty convincing. Should we call Chief Hurley and stop him from making a mistake with Bernie Maine?"

"Let's see if the money's here first," I said.

Instead of sliding into the dirt on my next lunge, the shovel in my hands hit something hard.

Maddy heard it, too. "Is that what I'm hoping it is?" she asked.

"There's only one way to find out." I got on my knees and reached down into the hole. It took ten seconds, but I finally found something I could pull up on. When we wrestled the object out of the hole, I realized that it was an old suitcase, and from the look of it, it hadn't been buried that long.

I was about to open it when I heard a man's voice behind me say, "Nicely done, ladies. I'll take that, if you don't mind."

It was Kenny Stout, and when I looked up at him in the light of the moon, I saw that he'd brought a shovel of his very own to the party.

"You didn't kill Grant, did you?" I asked. I hated to see my carefully reasoned solution to the crime fall apart just before I breathed my last breath.

"What? Of course not. I knew he took the money, though, and I figured that whoever killed him didn't have it. I broke into his place over there, but I didn't find a thing, so I thought I'd keep an eye on you two and see what you were able to come up with."

"But you had to know that something was buried here. Why else carry a shovel and pick around in your station wagon?"

"Truthfully? I was going to plant a flower bed," he said with a smile.

"But you rent."

"What can I say? I like a little color in my life. It just worked out that I had all the tools I needed with me when I spotted you two sneaking out of your house tonight."

"But you bought that huge footlocker," Maddy protested.

"Sure. I needed a new one so I could put some of my things in storage. Why? What did you think I bought it for?"

"We figured you were going to kill Samantha and bury her in it," I said.

That brought out a full laugh from him. "Are you kidding me? Why would I kill my meal ticket? Without her, I'm just an okay musician. She's the draw onstage, and we both know it."

"You know, it took a while, but it's finally nice to hear you admit it," Samantha said as she stepped out of the shadows behind him.

The moonlight revealed the gun in her hand, and I felt little consolation knowing that I'd been right about who had killed Grant Whitmore after all.

"How did you find us?" I asked her. "And why did you even come looking for us in the first place?"

"I spotted your pizza boy following me earlier today," she said. "He wasn't very clever about it, so it wasn't all that hard to do. I had a hunch that something was up, so as soon as he left my apartment, I began trailing Kenny." She looked at her ex-husband and added, "You're too easy. You know that, don't you? There were two of us on your tail at one point, and you didn't see either one of us."

"Why were you following *me?*" he asked.

"I was going to kill you, of course," she answered. By the tone of her voice, she could have just as easily said that she was going to take him out to dinner, and I realized that something in Samantha must have snapped. "I'm leaving the country, and I wasn't about to let you think that you ran me off. You bullied me onstage *and* offstage in our marriage, but I was going to get the final say."

"What about us?" Maddy asked her.

"Sorry, but you're just collateral damage from friendly fire."

"Surely you can't expect to get away with killing all three of us," I said.

"Four, actually. Don't forget Grant. That was a mistake, actually."

"Killing him? I'd think so," Maddy said.

I tried to figure out what chance we had of stopping her as she spoke. Should I throw my shovel at her like a spear? She was far enough away from us that I doubted I'd be able to do any damage. How about if I shouted out for help? No, the neighborhood was as dead as we were about to be if we didn't do something quickly.

"No, I don't regret that, but I do wish that I'd found the money he stole first." Then she looked down at the dirty suitcase. "I see you've done that for me, though. Why don't you be a good girl and toss it over here to me," she demanded.

"I'm not strong enough," I said, though I probably could have managed it. I wanted her to come closer so I'd have a chance of using it as a weapon. "Whatever is in there is weighing it down."

She didn't fall for the trap, though.

"Kenny, make yourself useful. Drop your shovel, get the suitcase, and bring it to me. You might not have done what I asked you to while we were married, but you have a little more incentive to make me happy right now, wouldn't you say?"

Kenny dropped his shovel as he said, "Samantha, you'll never get away with this."

"As a matter of fact, I believe that I will. Now, do as I say!"

Kenny walked over to the suitcase, picked it up, and then started toward his ex-wife with it.

When he was six feet away, she ordered, "That's far enough. Drop it right there."

Instead of doing as he was told, though, Kenny held the suitcase up as a shield in front of his body and ran straight at her. What was the fool trying to do?

Samantha didn't even hesitate. She shot him from two feet away, and he crumpled at her feet.

I knew then that if there was any doubt before, it was gone now.

We were all about to die.

While Samantha looked down at her ex-husband with a sick grin on her face, it was time for action. I might be about to die, but I wasn't going down without a fight.

I threw my shovel at her with everything I had.

Maddy didn't throw her pick, though.

She, too, ran straight at Samantha, the pick held high over her head.

"No!" I shouted just as Samantha looked up.

Maddy's pick left her hands in that instant, turning end over end as it flew toward Samantha's chest.

My shovel hit a glancing blow off her arm, but unfortunately, it wasn't the one holding the gun.

Maddy's aim with the pick was truer than mine, though. It sank into Samantha's shoulder, and the gun flew up into the air as the murderer fell to the ground.

As I rushed toward the weapon to keep Samantha from recovering it, we heard a voice from the house call out, "What's going on out there? I'm going to call the police."

"Do that," I said as I reached down and picked up the gun.

"Eleanor, is that you? What's going on?" Rebecca asked.

"There's too much to even tell you right now," I said as I pulled out my own phone and dialed 911.

I had a lot to say, and I wanted to have to say it only once.

Chapter 19

"Tell it to me one more time, from the beginning," Chief Hurley ordered as Maddy and I sat in his office an hour after the confrontation had taken place.

"Our story's not going to change," I said. "Have they counted the money yet? Is the entire hundred and fifty grand that went missing there?"

"It's with the forensic accountant right now," he said. "She'll let me know when she gets a final count. I don't envy her the mess the courts will have on their hands, figuring out who gets what after the trial is over." The police chief glanced over at Maddy and added, "If any of it is even coming to you, I wouldn't count on seeing it within the next ten years."

"I'm not holding my breath," she said. "Just knowing that Sharon thought so much of me is enough of an inheritance for me." Maddy added with a grin, "Besides, getting Bob off the hook is really all the payment I need. Did you ever catch up with Bernie Maine?"

"We found him, all right," Chief Hurley admitted. "We had to let him go, though, given Samantha's confession." He looked down at his notes and then shut off the video camera and tape recorder he had running before he spoke again. "When did you two figure it out?" he asked softly.

"Don't give us too much credit. We didn't get it until about two minutes before Samantha showed up," I explained. "We were still digging the hole when we realized that she was the only one of our suspects who planned to run. She must have known how it would look, though, because she orchestrated a pretty elaborate cover for it from the first moment we saw her after the murder. She didn't let it rest with that, though."

The chief nodded. "If we didn't go after Kenny, she was ready to frame Bernie Maine. Planting Grant's bloodstained wallet at Maine's place was pretty brilliant."

"I guess it was, but I had to think about the evil in that woman's heart. She seemed so nonchalant when she threatened to kill us. It was as though it didn't matter to her one way or the other what happened to any of us," I said.

"Did she say why she killed Grant?" he asked.

"No, but it's not hard to figure out. He stole from her, broke her heart, and then wouldn't take her back again once he was free of Vivian. It pushed her over the edge, and she snapped," Maddy said.

"I hope she doesn't try an insanity defense," the chief said.

"I'm not so sure that it's not appropriate in this case," I said. "Is she talking now?"

"No, she's still in surgery."

"How badly did I hurt her?" Maddy asked.

"The doctors said that none of the damage is permanent, but she's going to be in some pretty fierce pain when she wakes up."

"Since she just tried to kill all of us, I believe that I can live with that," Maddy said.

"I've got enough here," the chief said as he looked back down at his notes. "If you'd like, you two are free to go now."

"Thanks, Chief," I said.

Out in the hallway, I was about to say something to Maddy when Bob appeared out of nowhere and wrapped her in his arms. To my delight, David did the same with me. After a few minutes, we all managed to pull ourselves free.

"Hey, guys, it's okay. We're fine. Really," I reassured them.

"We were pretty worried about you," David said. "You should have called us."

"We managed on our own okay, but we appreciate the offer," I said as I kissed his cheek. "I will admit that it was a little more than we bargained for in the end."

Bob looked at Maddy and said, "I can't believe that I almost lost you. Did you really throw a pick-ax at Samantha Stout? I heard that you wrecked her shoulder pretty thoroughly."

"She got lucky. I was trying to bring her down completely," Maddy admitted. "But I never could have done it if Eleanor hadn't thrown her shovel at Samantha first. It was enough to distract her for the few seconds I needed to strike out."

"And let's not forget Kenny's part in this. He's the one who distracted her long enough to let me do that. How is he, by the way?"

"He got hit in the thigh, but the doctors think he's going to be just fine, though he'll probably have a limp for a while," Bob said.

"Good enough," I said. "Remind me to bring him a pizza here when he's able to eat outside food. The man's still a bully and a cad, but he saved our lives, and I'm not about to forget that."

"I think it was more a matter of self-preservation, when you think about it," Maddy said.

"Hey, whatever his motivations were, we couldn't have done what we did if he hadn't been crazy enough to run straight at a woman with a hand-gun," I said. As I turned to Bob and David, I asked, "So, are you two ready to get out of here?"

David nodded. "We are, but we're probably all

too wired to sleep. Is anybody else up for a cup of coffee and a piece of pie?"

"I could eat something after I get cleaned up first," Maddy said with a grin as she looked at her clay-stained clothing, and I agreed as I followed the three of them out of the police station.

It had been a close call tonight, closer than I would have ever liked, but we'd come through the other side with nothing more than a few blisters from digging, a pretty solid scare, and another story to tell someday. I was particularly proud of my sister for the way that she'd acted. When Kenny had taken her stun gun from her, I'd been worried that it would kill her willingness and ability to defend herself, but she'd proven to everyone, and most importantly, to herself, that when the stakes really mattered, she was fearless and ready to take bold action. In a very real way, Samantha Stout had given Maddy a valuable opportunity to prove to herself that she had what it took to stand up and be counted when it mattered most.

Not that any of us would ever thank the crazy woman for it.

As for me, I was looking forward to getting home, cleaning up, and then going out with the three people in the world I loved the most, to celebrate our lives and what tomorrow might hold for each of us.

It was the perfect way to end the day and another period of turmoil in all our lives.

RECIPES FOR CHEESE STICKS AND MINI CALZONES

Sometimes when I'm making pizza, I find that I have extra dough. Instead of throwing anything away, I like to see how creative I can be when it comes to using up my ingredients to the last bit, so these treats were born.

The first step is taking some dough, rolling it out to a quarter-inch thickness, and cutting it into strips about three inches long, if the amount of dough allows it. Then I work directly into the dough whatever cheese I have on hand. Parmesan cheese works great, and so do mozzarella, cheddar, and just about any cheese you like with your pizzas, if they are grated finely enough to be incorporated into the dough.

Next, I braid these strips together loosely and then bake them in my pizza oven. These cook fairly quickly, so it's a good idea to keep an eye on them. When they are browned on top, pull them out and add a dusting of Parmesan. Your regular pizza sauce makes a great dipping sauce for these sticks, and chances are, you still have some on hand.

You can also make a dessert version of these sticks by substituting a little diced butter and diced apple or pear for the cheese, dusting the assembled braids with cinnamon and sugar, and baking. These braids will be a little more difficult to work with, but they are a delightful dessert to go along with your pizza.

Finally, if I have enough dough, I like to make mini calzones out of the same ingredients. Roll the dough out, top with some pizza sauce and your favorite toppings and cheeses, wet the edge of one side of the dough before folding the other side over, and bake.

You can also make dessert calzones this way. One easy way I've found is to use canned apple pie filling or canned cherry pie filling. Simply fold the dough over the fruit filling and bake.

As an added treat, try incorporating pineapple and mozzarella into the savory mini calzones, and pineapple with cinnamon sugar into the sweet ones. You'll be amazed by how great the pineapple tastes in both versions.

Grab These Cozy Mysteries
from
Kensington Books

Follow P.I. Savannah Reid
with
G.A. McKevett

Available Wherever Books Are Sold!

All available as e-books, too!

Visit our website at **www.kensingtonbooks.com**